THE

DEEP SEA

DIVER'S

SYNDROME

THE

DEEP SEA

DIVER'S

SYNDROME

a novel

SERGE BRUSSOLO

Translated by
EDWARD GAUVIN

MELVILLE HOUSE
BROOKLYN · LONDON

THE DEEP SEA DIVER'S SYNDROME

Originally published by Les Éditions DENOËL
as *Le syndrome du scaphandrier*
Copyright © 1992 by Éditions DENOËL

Translation copyright © 2016 by Edward Gauvin

First Melville House printing: January 2016

Melville House Publishing   8 Blackstock Mews
             46 John Street   and   Islington
          Brooklyn, NY 11201   London N4 2BT

mhpbooks.com   facebook.com/mhpbooks   @melvillehouse

Library of Congress Cataloging-in-Publication Data
Names: Brussolo, Serge, 1951– | Gauvin, Edward, translator.
Title: The deep sea diver's syndrome : a novel / Serge Brussolo ;
    translated by Edward Gauvin.
Other titles: *Syndrome du scaphandrier*. English
Description: Brooklyn, NY : Melville House, [2016]
Identifiers: LCCN 2015032079 | ISBN 9781612194684
    (hardback) | ISBN 9781612194691 (ebook)
Subjects: LCSH: Dreams—Fiction. | Science fiction. | BISAC:
    FICTION / Science Fiction / Adventure. | FICTION / Literary.
Classification: LCC PQ2662.R8565 S9613 2016 | DDC
    843/.914—dc23
LC record available at http://lccn.loc.gov/2015032079

Printed in the United States of America

10 9 8 7 6 5 4 3 2 1

With support from

Centre national   du livre

THE

DEEP SEA

DIVER'S

SYNDROME

[1]

Robbery in Deep Water

. . . the long, black, oily car clung to the sidewalk. Like a giant wet rubbery leech fastened to the foot of the building, siphoning blood from the façade, slowly gorging on the vital fluid flushing the pink marble . . . Would the structure shrivel up, wither away? Instinctively, David reached out for the car door to make sure the metal wasn't going soft. He checked himself just in time. Rule number one: keep fleeting impressions from blossoming into full-blown fantasies. A moment's inattention and images seized the chance to sink roots, proliferating at incredible speed—like tropical plants that, no sooner slashed, sprouted back, stalks dripping sap, amputees already reanimating . . .

. . . but still the long, black, oily car had something of the circling shark to it. Headlights like eyes unsettling in their steadiness, chrome bumpers like giant teeth that could mangle any prey.

David felt the vehicle's texture altering around him as the image gained materiality. Inside, it stank of fish, the seat leather slowly growing scales. The air outside smelled of kelp, tidal scum foaming in the gutters . . .

"Stability issues," Nadia muttered without looking at him. "You're too nervous." The fish reek was unbearable now. David leaned toward the door. The trunk and fender were halfway to becoming a huge caudal fin. The bodywork was beginning to bristle with sharp, tiny scales, a kind of wet leather that made his fingers prickle just looking at it. *I'm being stupid.* The young man forced himself to control his thoughts. *This car looks nothing like a shark. Nothing.* He had to pull himself together fast, because the view down the street was changing too, in keeping with the car's mutations. The great white façade of the museum was looking more like a chalk cliff all the time, and the massive statues lining the front steps like . . . reefs. Timid waves were rising from the gutters to lick and lap at the first steps, dragging seaweed and driftwood in their wake. David blinked. The marble stairs were slowly eroding, the steps sagging, soft as sand. They melted into each other, forming a small, very white beach in the pale light of a full moon.

"Fix your stability," Nadia said again. There was always a catch in that husky voice of hers. It was a tremendous effort for David to turn and look at the young woman. She'd hid her fiery red hair under a longshoreman's cap and turned up the collar of her leather jacket to look more mannish, but her full lips with their ever-weary pout gave her away. "Quit fucking around," she grumbled. "I'm about to turn into a mermaid here. I can't feel my feet anymore." She tried to laugh, but fear cut through the joke.

She threw him a wild glance. "What's with you tonight? This was supposed to be an easy job!"

David moved his tongue around, but could not manage to form a word. If the car turned into a shark, they'd both wind up trapped in its belly, in danger of being dissolved by stomach acid, right? *It's a car*, he chanted, a mantra. *Just a car.* To convince himself, he began reciting tech specs from the handbook: top speed, miles per gallon city and highway—

The scales subsided; the trunk lost its finlike look. A car, a good old low-slung sports coupe that hugged the ground like greased lightning, quick as an attacking shark—*No! Don't start!*

He turned his attention to the street, empty at this late hour. The museum statues stood guard along the sidewalk, sentries fossilized by fatigue. The tall façade of white marble unpleasantly intensified the streetlight glow. The jewelry boutique was on the other side of the square, a plush little setting for a window display with inch-thick glass proof against any explosive. David plunged his hand into the pocket of his leather jacket, came up with a big starchy handkerchief, and dried his sweaty palms. What time was it? He checked his diving watch. Its digital display blinked: *Depth 3,300 feet.* Three thousand was enough to guarantee a good chance at success. He wasn't going any deeper tonight, he could tell; he was too light. He hadn't plunged into the water hard enough. His feet lacked that lead-soled shoe feeling that had heralded the vertiginous descents of his glory days. Still, three thousand feet wasn't bad. Instinctively, he leaned toward the windshield to check out the sky, almost expecting to see columns of bubbles rising into the air.

"You taking off?" Nadia asked, worried. He nodded. The

depth gauge showed *3,295*, which meant the ascent had begun; the longer he waited, the worse his working conditions would get. He had to act now. "Take a consistency pill," Nadia suggested, handing him an unlabeled brass tube. David popped the top. A blue pill fell into the hollow of his palm. He swallowed it. "Remember," Nadia whispered, "three's the limit."

He made no reply. He was well aware of the dosage. He took a great gulp of air, grabbed the metal briefcase on the backseat, and got out. He did not emerge from the jaws of a massive fish; the car had completely reverted to its original shape. As Nadia slid into the driver's seat, he crossed the square, trying to come down hard on the cobblestones. But the clack of his heels lacked sharpness, revealing the material weakening of the world around him. It was a direct result of the ascent. As he drew closer to the surface, sounds would fade away, vases break in silence, the most devastating explosions morph into sneezes . . . He checked the depth gauge, worried: *3,290 feet*. A slow but irreversible ascent. He'd clearly observed the various symptoms right before his dive: restless legs, too-dry eyeballs that his eyelids painfully chafed, sweaty palms he tried to wipe on his sheets . . .

His metal heels struck the cobblestones with no greater sound than the distant echo of a tiny bell. He was tempted to punch the rounded belly of the briefcase to make it ring like a gong, but decided against it, less from fear of drawing attention than from dread of being met with only an alarmingly paltry noise. He looked up again at the sky—at the surface. The moon's silver disk stood out against the night. Once, not far from the moon, he'd glimpsed the hull of a ship at anchor . . . even fish. Fish, swimming among the chimney tops overhead. He had to stop thinking about these things; all they did was hasten the ascent. With a firm step he made for the boutique, whose window gave off a greenish glow in the dark. The pearls and tiaras behind the bastion of reinforced glass seemed half-buried in the silt. David blinked. No, not silt, cushions, just green velvet cushions. At any rate, the consistency pill would be kicking in any minute now. He had to seize that brief window and go to work. He approached the front door, which led to a kind of airlock where customers were detained for a moment before being allowed into the boutique. Once you had entered that cramped booth, a physiognomist went to work, scrutinizing you from head to toe through the glass, assessing your "financial standing" from tiny signs. If your shoes were nice, but alas, too new, that was condemnation enough; ditto for gems and diamonds of inadequate carat. Then a voice would come through the tinny speaker: "Sorry, sir, but perhaps you have the wrong address? There's nothing in this store for you." Humiliated, disgraced, you had no choice but to turn tail and shuffle from the vestibule like some indigestible scrap rejected by a healthy organism. David dug around in his pocket, looking for the big key with the complicated blade for the first door. It hadn't been too hard to come by, since getting past the first door wasn't really getting into the boutique. Once you set foot in that airlock, that exam room—then, and only then, did things get serious. The key turned in the asterisk-shaped keyhole with a well-oiled click. A tiny light went on in the jamb of brushed steel. David put his hand on the glass and pushed. His fingerprints came off as little smiling faces, caricatures with a strong resemblance to his own features. It was as if each finger-tip were a rubber stamp for certifying bureaucratic documents. He checked out his right hand. At the tip of his index finger he made out a faithfully engraved intaglio portrait of himself. He shrugged. None of this was important. Merely a rudimentary manifestation of guilt; he shouldn't let this kind of thing slow him down—not even if, in a few minutes, his sweat went fluorescent like it had two months ago. He'd seen it all. During an earlier dive, his fingers had stubbornly persisted in leaving his name and address in black ink on every surface he must have touched. He entered the airlock; the door shut automatically behind him. The slightest mistake and he'd find himself a prisoner of the booth, which also served to trap burglars beating a retreat. It was a fool-proof cell with an unpleasant foretaste of prison to it. With the same key as before, David opened a panel set into the wall to his left, exposing a pane of frosted glass and an eyepiece that immediately lit up: two ultrasensitive scanners, palm print and retinal. They'd been programmed for the shop owner's right hand and left eye. The intrusion of any organs not matching the saved patterns would immediately set off every alarm in the store, and deadbolt the airlock doors on any stranger foolhardy enough to try the scanners. David set the metallic briefcase on the floor, popped the clasps, and lifted the lid. This was always a delicate moment—when he had to overcome his disgust. It was an effort to unfold the bloodstained napkin that held the jeweler's severed hand. Nadia had done a clean job, with her expertise as a former army nurse. She'd amputated at the wrist without resorting to the bone saw she kept in her kit. "Better this way," she often said.

"He'll have a nice clean stump, with no bone pain later." David was quite certain that given the time, she would've gone so far as to stitch her victim up herself, from a sense of professional duty. He, for one, never watched the operations. He'd go into the next room, smoke a cigar, try to ignore the metallic sounds of the instruments. Nadia always put her patients under. She worked in white scrubs, as if presiding at an actual hospital. Her skill was astounding; she could've taught a real surgeon a trick or two. She worked without breaking a sweat, while the mere sound of a scalpel striking the edge of the stainless steel pan made David clammy all over with perspiration . . .

The square of frosted glass gave off a blinding white light, demanding that the first phase of the identification process begin immediately. If no hand was placed on its surface in thirty seconds, it would set off a general alarm. Finally overcoming his disgust, David grabbed the hunk of flesh by its sticky end and slapped the palm on the plate. It hit the glass with the wet smack of a bird flying into a window. The machine purred, gathering information. The retinal scanner blinked in turn, betraying its impatience. With his free hand, David uncorked the vial where Nadia had dropped the jeweler's left eye, so carefully enucleated an hour ago. He swore. The gelatinous ball was slippery between his fingers. He didn't dare squeeze, for fear of popping it. One false move, and he'd find himself imprisoned in the airlock, reduced to waiting helplessly for the police. Silently counting off the seconds, he finally got control of the eyeball and raised it gently to the level of the glowing lens. He knew he had to get it right side up; Nadia had made him practice the action at length, showing him how to tell if the organ was upside down from a few markers on the back. Fingers trembling, he held the ocular orb up to the black rubber eyepiece. The machine hummed again, and then the door to the boutique unlocked with a hiss of hydraulic pistons. David wrapped the body parts in the bloodstained handkerchief, stowed it in the briefcase, and entered the boutique. His legs felt weak, and he would have given anything for a glass of whisky. Getting in had been accomplished with extraordinary consistency—no loss of control—and in his delight, he passed up a glance at his depth gauge. The pill had made his mouth pasty and numbed the underside of his tongue. To double-check action of the drug, he slammed the big key on a showcase full of necklaces. This time, the impact produced a clear, shapely tinkling sound: no ebbing or wobbling. Sometimes noises would go into an endless quaver like a cassette tape run too slow. That was usually a bad sign. He slammed the showcase again, savoring the crisp clink attesting to the solidity of the world around him. He crossed the boutique without glancing at the jewelry on display. What he'd come for was always deep in a safe in back, far from prying customers. Another fundamental rule, not to be argued with. No matter the shop, the safe was always the same: fat, black, oafish, and anachronistic, with a huge dial in the middle of the door. A forbidding cube that never rang hollow, that no crane could have lifted or budged so much as an inch. The perfect safe . . . Once in back, he reached a door with a brass plate that said PRIVATE. The big key let him in. Behind it was a sitting room with heavy red draperies, cluttered with bronzes and sculptures. The safe was at the very back of the room, its big black door guarding the entrance to a forbidden citadel. David took his stethoscope from the briefcase and began sounding out the door. The dial rattled, amplified by his instrument. David focused on the clicks rising from the cast iron. Now, more than ever, he needed a musician's ear. Abruptly incongruous images formed in his mind, and he saw himself in a doctor's office, leaning over the abdomen of an obese patient. As if following suit, the safe let out a burp, painfully vibrating the stethoscope's diaphragm. *Enough!* David thought, as if that naïve magic word were all it took to restore order. Now a great big heart was beating behind the reinforced door, making a dreadful, unbearable racket, masking the clicking of the dial. Then the safe began saying, "33 . . . 33 . . . 33 . . ." with the regularity of a clock bent on running forever. David tore the stethoscope from his ears and swallowed another consistency pill. He was perspiring freely now; sweat trickled in an unbroken stream from his armpits. Without thinking, he patted his jacket pocket, where he kept a dime bag of realism powder. He could sniff it on the glass-topped desk right here and now, but even though the powder curbed onei-ric drift, it also hastened the ascent: a side effect he had to keep in mind. He fingered the bag, hesitating. Too much realism and he could take off right in the middle of the heist. He didn't relish the prospect. Better to try to push forward through the parasitic drift, keeping his eye on the prize. He turned back to the safe and began listening again. At first all he heard through the chestpiece was intestinal gurgling, and he had to strain his ears to make out the faint clicking of the dial as it turned. *Click . . . click . . . clack!* said the lock. *Screw you!* the chorus of tumblers retorted. *Take your hardware and scram!* added the armor plating. They were chanting in rhythm, spinning off endless variations on their simple theme, the singsong harmoniously dovetailing like an operetta with a strangely metallic aftertaste. Each click of the dial was another note the iron choir fell in tune with. David shrank back, his face slick. He mopped his forehead and palms with the starchy handkerchief. A scratching sound from the desk made him turn around. With some anxiety, he saw the jeweler's severed hand had escaped from the briefcase and crawled across the blotter adorning the desktop. It had grabbed a pen and was now writing in large, tremulous letters, *My dear man, you'll get nowhere tonight. Beat it before the police surround the building.* The eyeball was floating in the air, peering at the statues and bronzes; sometimes it swooped down and froze over the ledgers, hovering like a helicopter. David pressed his forehead against the safe's icy door. He couldn't back out; it was an easy job. Nadia had said so. Besides, there was no way he could go back up empty-handed; these last few weeks he'd already dived three times without bringing anything back. If this unlucky streak dragged on, they'd soon be accusing him of incompetence. They'd even go so far as to claim his powers were wearing out. *I'm rising*, he thought as panic seeped in. *Yes, we're going up*, the severed hand feverishly scribbled on the blotter. *Fifth floor: women's lingerie, silken trifles; sixth floor, children's department*—frantically, David grabbed the dial. The door to the safe let out a loud sigh. *Why, Doctor, what icy hands you have!* the lock snickered. *I'm too light*, thought David, *I'm flying upwards. It's like my feet aren't even on the ground anymore. My pockets are full of bubbles.* Echoing this last thought, a heavy cut-glass inkwell rose from the desk, wafting gently over the books and the clock. As a phenomenon, weightlessness meant the world of the job was in the process of losing its initial density. Objects hollowed, grew friable, fragile as papier-mâché. A thick leather-bound tome took flight next, joining the inkwell. David touched the door. The metal had changed textures too; now it felt like something between terra-cotta and stucco. *Might as well.* David steeled himself. *What are you waiting for?* He made a fist, drew it back, and punched the safe with all his might, as if trying to flatten a giant in an unfair match. There was an eggshell crack as his fist hit the steel door. Off-balance, he fell into the cube, his arm shoulder-deep inside the safe. His fingers blindly groped the shelves, fumbled crunching bagfuls of loose stones. He came across bags like that in every heist; the psychologist said it was negative thinking. Objects with a precise shape, however convoluted, would've been worth more. The bags invariably meant a small take. He grabbed them anyway.

His heart was beating way too fast. The veins in his left arm were beginning to ache, a painful blister throbbing on his wrist, right over his pulse. He leaned on the desk to catch his breath. He had to stay cool in the face of a nightmare, or else the dream would eject him without regard for decompression stops. He mastered his breathing. If he gave in to the nightmare, the excess of anxiety would result in a brutal awakening as his consciousness tried to flee unbearable images by snapping back to reality. If he wasn't careful, he'd take off right from where he was standing, literally sucked up toward the surface. He'd rise straight into the air, clothes and shoes tearing away, punch through the ceiling and the whole building like an arrow through a lump of clay . . . he'd lived through it once or twice before, and it was a horrible memory. The feeling of suddenly becoming a human cannonball, tearing head-first at the most terrifying obstacles: walls, floorboards, ceilings, rafters, roofs . . . Each time he was sure his skull would burst open at the next impact, and even though that never happened, hurtling through buildings of slime was still a disgusting experience. When the dream stopped short, the structure of things weakened, the hardest materials took on an ectoplasmic consistency like raw egg whites or jellyfish. He'd had to make his way through that cloacal mire, arms over his head to streamline his ascent, mouth clamped shut to keep from gulping down the gelatinous substance of a de-composing dream . . .

Nightmare ejected you without a care for the demands of your mission, subjecting you to the stress of an emergency pro-cedure that left you empty-handed. Whenever it happened, the ascent was too swift to hang on to your haul. Jewels, stacks of bills, bags of precious stones—the pressure inevitably tore them from your grip. Your clothes split at the seams, you felt in every abused joint like you'd been torn apart by wild horses. And then there was the friction of water on your body: a pleasant silken caress that grew ever more painful as the speed increased. When you woke up, your skin was red as if it'd been sandpapered, with open wounds where the friction had been greatest.

David forced himself to breathe slowly. Clutching the bags of diamonds to his chest, he groped his way toward another consis-tency pill. He slipped it from the tube onto his tongue, swallowing to force out saliva and dissolve it. Three pills: he'd reached the maximum dosage. Any more and he was in danger of what divers

called *the bell*: an extreme inertia that slowed your every move
and forced you to make countless calculations before lifting so
much as a finger. In his early days, David had made that mistake
once or twice; he'd found himself literally paralyzed by a maniacal
obsession with measurements. While sitting in an armchair, he'd
suddenly been plagued by an insane need to determine at once the
exact resistance the seat offered the weight of his body; then to derive the equation governing the translocatory motion that would
take him from the armchair to the door. After that, he'd furiously
calculated the pressure his fingers exerted on every square inch of
the porcelain knob. He'd wound up abysmally lost in estimating
the perimeter and volume of the room, trying to determine the specific resistances of the materials that composed it. He woke just as
he was beginning a new series of computations to ascertain with
the greatest possible precision the number of years—centuries?—
it would take rain to erode the walls and reduce them to the thick-
ness of rolling papers. The bell was a holy terror. A kind of mental
vertigo that hurled you down a well of mathematical formulae
and equations. Three pills was really the max, if you didn't want
your brain to turn into a crazed calculator.

His heart was beating almost normally now. The punctured
safe was no longer singing. Only the severed hand kept twitching
on the blotter. Suddenly it threw itself at David, trying to claw his
face, put out an eye. He flung it aside with the back of his hand
and hurried from the room. He was almost to the airlock when he
remembered he needed the body parts to get through it again. He
eyed the metal plate that concealed the two scanners. If he wanted
to get out of the boutique, he'd have to go through the exact same

steps he'd used to get in. He needed what Nadia had removed from the anesthetized jeweler. The image came back to him: the man reclining in a barber's chair, all leather and upholstery tacks (a rich man's fancy), with his oddly truncated arm wrapped in a towel, and a gauze plug stuffed in his empty eye socket like an out-of-place cork. "He didn't feel a thing," Nadia had said. "I left him instructions for when he wakes up, and a little something for the pain." But where was the hand now? And the eye?

David retraced his steps. The severed hand was scratching at the blotter like a mad beast, raising a cloud of pink dust. The eye was floating high above between the pendants of the chandelier. "C'mere!" David ordered stupidly, taking a step forward. The hand sprang from the desk at once and scuttled under a chest of drawers. David got up on a chair to try to grab the eye, but it hugged the ceiling, remaining out of reach. He took another swipe, but the legs of the chair went rubbery and the seat tore under his weight, throwing him to the ground. The back of his neck struck the corner of the desk, but it was painless; even the desk was now soft as marshmallow. The deterioration was getting worse. He checked his watch. The glowing face read *1,650 feet*. He had to get out of the shop at any cost; that was how things worked. If he woke up before he got away, he'd lose the haul and surface empty-handed. Violent blows shook the shop window behind him. He turned, nervous: it was Nadia, slamming the armored glass with both fists to get his attention. "I can't get out!" he yelled, exaggerating the words so she could read his lips. "I lost the eye and the hand." Nadia puckered up, blew mist on the glass, and began writing something backwards. It was slow going, and she messed up a few letters, but soon David could make it out: *Doesn't matter for you now. Dream breaking up. You can make it through. More solid than me.*

Instinctively, David felt himself with his hands. She was right. Dreamers were always denser than the dream worlds they moved through. The difference was negligible when the dream was in full swing, but useful once things started falling apart.

"You can make it through!" Nadia was yelling on the other side. "You're more solid than the glass! C'mon!"

David started backing up to throw himself through the pane, but the fear of hurting himself stopped him cold. For a moment he had a vision of glass shards shredding his face, severing his carotid. No, he wouldn't make it; the shattered window's razor-sharp fragments would rip his throat open. He—

The howl of the alarm made him start. He realized the jeweler's hand must have set it off, just pressed a button hidden in a drawer, sending a signal straight to the nearest precinct. The alarm wailed like a cow being tortured . . . or a ship heading out to sea. David shut his eyes. He could smell the sea again, his feet were in the sand, and his hands were clutching pebbles . . . *No! Dammit! Not pebbles: uncut stones! Raw diamonds!*

Nadia's frenzied blows brought him to his senses. Her pale face was gleaming with sweat, and a lock of red hair fallen free from her cap streaked her forehead like blood. David backed up, gauging the window's solidity, the door's steel frame. At first glance it all seemed terribly solid, capable of withstanding even a truck at full speed without cracking. But that was just an illusion; he was much too close to the surface now for the dream world to stand up to the materiality of the dreamer. All he needed was a little speed and the glass would crack like the safe had just now . . . but what about the consistency pills? Wouldn't they help reinforce the density of the armored glass? In which case he was running smack into disaster. Nadia was still shouting, but he couldn't hear her anymore. The din of the alarm filled his ears. From sheer nerves, he kicked a sofa, which pulled back like a jellyfish. The jewels on display had an oily gleam, the pearls seemed to be melting like dabs of butter in the sun. He could afford to wait no longer. Clutching the bags of jewels to his chest, David tensed his muscles and dove headfirst through the glass, flying right over the display. In real life, he'd never have been able to pull off a stunt like that without winding up in traction, but in dreams his body rarely betrayed him. It was a well-oiled machine, ever faithful and reliable. Or almost . . .

The armored glass exploded the moment his skull hit it. The shards weren't sharp at all, and showered soundlessly onto the sidewalk. David rolled to a stop at Nadia's feet, his hair covered in crystalline dust. He spat out a few pieces of glass, noticing they left a minty aftertaste—maybe because of the greenish tint?

Nadia helped him back to his feet and dragged him toward the car. He barely felt her hand on his biceps. He wondered if the vehicle would bear his weight, or if he'd find himself sitting in the street. With the change in density, you had to be ready for anything.

"You're slow," Nadia groaned. "Did you take all your pills?"

"Yes," he confessed, getting gingerly into shotgun.

Nadia always took the wheel when it was time for the getaway.

As a diver steadily approaching wakefulness, he was afraid that at the first turn he'd tear the steering wheel right off the column with his increased density.

Nadia turned the key and pulled away just as the red lights showed up down the avenue. "Five-O," she said in a flat voice. David shriveled into the seat, not daring to move for fear of tearing through the vehicle. Luckily, the car held together, and the metal hadn't yet taken on the gelatinous look that signaled imminent waking.

"They're in hot pursuit," Nadia said, swinging the muscle car into an alley. The tires screeched at every turn, and the smell of burning rubber filled the car.

"Gonna be tight," the redhead muttered. "You took too long. Lost focus. Scared me. I should've come with you."

"You can't, you know that," David said softly, putting a hand on her arm. "That's now how it works. No changes to the ritual. I always have to go alone."

"That's why it keeps getting harder and harder. Your guilt's getting stronger. Somewhere deep down, you want to fail and come back empty-handed."

"No! That's not true!"

"C'mon!"

They were being shot at. Short bursts hammered the bodywork like a hail of ball bearings.

"We'll be OK," said Nadia, letting out a breath. "How deep are we?"

"Six hundred fifty feet," said David. "Waking any minute now."

"You take care of yourself up there, OK?" she whispered. "In the real world, I mean. Down here you always make it through, but up there . . . I'm scared whenever you go away. When will you come back down?"

"I don't know. In a week, if I can."

"That's a long time. When you're not here, I can't stop thinking about all the dangers waiting for you up there: diseases, accidents, hit and runs . . . what a terrible world."

"Terrible," David agreed, as the back windshield burst into pieces from the bullets. Nadia popped the glove box with one hand, grabbed a grenade, yanked the pin out with her teeth, and tossed it through the missing windshield.

"Diseases scare me the most," she said. "There's the—what do you call it again? The flu?"

The grenade exploded, tossing a police cruiser into the air. It landed heavily, blocking the street, belching out curls of smoke and flame.

"The flu's not that bad," said David. "Except if you're old. Don't worry about the flu."

He looked over his shoulder. Some cops were struggling to get clear of the twisted chassis. Others ran through the night frantically waving their arms, human torches, their screaming mouths the only dark spots on their bodies.

"You could die even if you never left the house," Nadia was saying. "You could slip on a bar of soap in the shower and crack your skull on the edge of the tub. Promise you won't shower too much? It doesn't matter if you're filthy. There are no smells in dreams."

No one was chasing them now. Nadia was still going pedal

to the metal to the edge of town. "We made it," she said, turning toward David with her eternally pained smile.

"It wasn't an easy job," he said sadly. "I have to do better next time. We can't keep going on like this."

"Don't let those people up there get to you," Nadia objected almost immediately. "You gotta be in tip-top shape to go lower than three thousand feet. No point tempting fate. If I hadn't been there tonight—"

The car was now rolling through a landscape of empty lots cluttered with unrecognizable shadows that stood out against the horizon like the plywood flats of a set. Nadia slowed down. The race was over now.

"Jorgo's coming for me," she murmured. "The cops can't trace this back to us, even if they find the car. I stole it this morning."

David opened the door and got out. The sun seemed too soft, jellyish. Nadia ran to his arms and pressed her lips to his. Her lips were always too hot, possessed of an unhealthy heat, a kind of chronic fever that alarmed him a little. David wanted to hold her close, but his muscles were melting away, losing their flattering volume. Suddenly his clothes hung loose on him, and it occurred to him he must look like a child in his father's raincoat. He tried to hunch forward and found his pecs had completely disappeared. He was nearing the surface; the process was irreversible. He knew if he stuck his hand in his pocket for his revolver (a huge Kass-Wrengler .357 magnum, blue steel with a ventilated rib and a stopping distance of . . .) he'd pull out something weird, even absurd: a water pistol, a suction dart gun for kids, maybe even a half-peeled banana. Or just a handful of sand. Or a tiny creature,

very fragile and almost dead. A kind of hairless kitten, blind and deaf . . . blind and deaf.

"I'm taking off," he gasped, grabbing Nadia by the shoulders. "Hold on to me!" But his fingers sank into the young woman's flesh, meeting no resistance. All he held now was a ghost.

"Remember!" Nadia cried, her face shrinking. "Diseases, accidents—don't stay up there too long!"

He wanted to say something in return, but the pull from the surface sucked him into the sky just as Jorgo came tearing through the empty lot on a motorcycle. He closed his eyes. He was waking up, and that wasn't the least bit reassuring.

[2]

Surface: Zero Point/ Apparent Calm

David was suffocating under sheets that covered him head to toe. He jerked instinctively, tossing them off. He hated coming back to reality under a shroud; it always made him feel like he'd woken from being buried alive only to slam his head against a coffin lid firmly nailed shut.

All he managed to emit—mouth gaping, neck muscles distended with effort—was a barely audible wail. He milled his arms and legs about in the middle of the bed in something like the crude breaststroke of a drowning man trying desperately to stay above water. *Swim!* cried a voice somewhere deep in his head. *Swim or you'll drown!* Awash in sweat, he tossed sheets and pillows around, dreading the cramps that might seize him any second now. He didn't want to drown, to sink like a rock into the mattress whose supple depths terrified him.

His eyelids were stuck shut as if sewn to his cheeks with the catgut of his lashes. He had to use his fingers to pry them open. His vision was still blurry, and he made out shapes in the room around him only through a flickering fog. The uniformly blue walls, the furniture and sheets of the same color, all contributed to an atmosphere of deep sea depths, and for a moment he thought he was still *down below* . . . he was beached on his back, sideways across the bed, legs hanging off the edge, still kicking weakly, from reflex. The blue sheets stank of sweat . . . and something else. An indefinable odor. *Electric.* Dumb, but it was the only word that came to mind. An electric smell. Something reminiscent of copper, ozone, the air after lightning. It was a clear sign he'd brought back something of value. This time he'd ascended without letting go of his booty from the depths. He wanted to stand up, but it was all he could do to roll over on his side. His head was spinning. There it was—*the thing*—at the foot of the bed, a prisoner of the crumpled sheets, palpitating faintly. He couldn't make out its exact shape. David reached out for it, but it was too far away. He sighed. He rarely ever saw them. He was the one who gave them life, but they always felt the need to hide beneath sheets, blankets, like frightened animals. What was it that scared them? Light? He'd carefully painted the room dark blue from floor to ceiling. Even the nightstand, the wardrobe, the rug were blue. When sun shone through the curtains, it was like being in a sea grotto. Very relaxing, conducive to sleep. *They* should have felt right at home . . .

"Are you awake?" Marianne said sharply, opening the door. "About time, the fridge was almost empty."

As usual, she had pulled her dark hair back into a teacher's strict bun and planted her thick tortoiseshell glasses on her straight nose. She was still young, and without the lips she always kept pursed, as if afraid of accidentally swallowing something, she might have been pretty. She came over to the bed, a thick novel in hand. David noted that she kept a finger in the book to mark the page. No, it wasn't a novel—rather, some technical study or clinical report. Marianne never read fiction. She leaned over the young man, took his pulse with a finger on his jugular. David pushed her away.

"How is it?" he whispered, pointing to the object struggling under the sheets. "Tell me."

Marianne shrugged and picked up a metal box from the floor. It was like a steel coffer for transporting cash. A complicated lock kept it shut.

David, trying once more to rise up on an elbow, begged, "Describe it to me—"

"Please," Marianne cut him off sharply. "Stop acting like a first-time mother. This second phase of the operation in no way involves you. You know quite well that mediums are advised against maintaining the slightest emotional connection with their products. Close your eyes and let me do my work."

Deftly she lifted the covers, grabbed the thing, and slipped it into the steel box. Its lock clicked like a gun being cocked. When she dropped the sheet again, David saw she was wearing gloves of surgical rubber. He strained to hear a cry, a whimper, some tiny sob from the coffer, but there was nothing. They were said to be mute, to neither speak nor sing, but how could you ever really tell? Marianne came and sat beside him for his checkup.

"You were bleeding," she said coldly, wiping around his mouth and chest. "I'm getting the feeling that materialization is becoming harder and harder for you. And your object was quite small."

"But is it beautiful?" David asked, pushing away the blood-flecked compress.

"I'm not authorized to evaluate the artistic qualities of dream objects," the young woman replied at once. "I simply see to the medical side of the work. Relax, and let me do your physical. Did you feel any pain on waking?"

"No," David lied, "the ascent wasn't any harder than usual."

Marianne pursed her lips in annoyance. She hated diving slang. Words like *ascent, decompression, deep-sea* made her furious. In her small, precise handwriting, she set about noting her patient's heart rate, blood pressure, reflexes. Atop the medical chart he could read: *David Sarella. Medium materializing ectoplasms of persistent duration. Date of entry into service . . .*

How many days had she spent in the apartment, waiting for him to emerge from sleep, to . . . "ascend"? Every time David decided to dive, she came over with her baggage, her severe-looking raincoat, and camped out on the very premises of the operation. That little black suitcase of hers—how he loathed it! The well-waxed suitcase of a priest, a plainclothes nun. He knew she always brought sheets, never trusting the cleanliness of his own. She would set up shop with her outmoded travel clock, probably passed down from some provincial aunt, her toiletries, her little slippers in their embroidered pouch. She perched the edges of her buttocks on the edges of chairs, eating with her own cutlery, drinking from a silver tumbler engraved with her initials. David had the hardest time picturing her sleeping in the guest room. Did she circle the bed for hours before deciding to go to sleep, an eye out for germs swarming in the folds of the pillowcase? As he, the professional dreamer, lost consciousness, she was free to come and go as she pleased in the old apartment: opening drawers, leafing through old letters, examining photos. She probably conducted her sneaky little rummagings with her fingertips, hands carefully gloved in surgical rubber, for fear of disturbing some virus dozing in the corner of a shelf.

As usual, David began in a glum voice to recount the twists and turns of his dream, which Marianne noted on the routine form. He spoke, his mind elsewhere. Through a part in Marianne's white lab coat, he could make out a big, shapeless sweater and a threadbare gray skirt. He'd barely said a dozen words before she interrupted him with an exasperated click of her tongue.

"I've asked you before to refrain from using that vocabulary with me," she said, stabbing the notebook with her pencil as if she wished to wound it. "Consistency pills, realism powder—they don't exist. They're inventions of your subconscious, symbolic warning signs. You know quite well you didn't ingest any pills. Try to keep in mind that what happens 'down below' has no existence in reality. There is no down below. Don't go lending these fantasies any substance, or you'll wind up a schizophrenic. The police pursuing you were simply a manifestation of your guilt. This . . . Nadia, on the other hand, is symbolic of your negative impulses. She's a bad example, urging you to commit crimes. She's the secret leader of a gang you think you lead—which you like, since in feeling forced to obey her, you feel freed from ordinary moral obligations. In a way, she clears you in your own eyes. You can claim you're only following orders."

"But Nadia—" David tried to object.

"That's enough!" Marianne hissed, stabbing the notebook again. "Keep this up and you'll wind up confusing dreams and reality, which is what happens to old dreamers. I believe that among yourselves, you call it 'the bends'—see, I'm familiar with your jargon. Be careful, David. I repeat: *there is no down below*. The whole break-in scenario is just a ritual, something that helps you do your work, a kind of magic formula that allows you to concentrate. Some dreamers imagine themselves on safari, hunting a mythical creature; others are climbing an unconquered peak in search of some undiscovered mineral. Still others explore space in a rocket, landing on unknown planets. I could go on; examples abound. All these patterns stem directly from a childhood stock of images. They must not be romanticized."

David closed his eyes. Her incessant recommendations wearied him. He had to put up with them every time he surfaced, and every time Marianne reeled them off in the same reproving voice of a teacher tired of lecturing a backward student. These repetitive sermons never managed to weaken the reality of the world below in his mind. How could Marianne, who'd never taken the plunge herself, be so adamant about it? David could still taste Nadia's lips on his own, and remembered precisely the pattern of freckles on her cheeks. How could he have invented all those details? The badly stitched rip that split her jacket by her left shoulder. Jorgo's good old motorcycle—always the same one, its gas tank salvaged from an old Rolls . . . Mere dreams had no respect for such consistency of detail. In an ordinary dream, Nadia would've switched back and forth from being a blonde to a brunette. Her name and face would've changed over the course of a heist; she would've been multiple women at the same time. Marianne could go on spitefully stabbing her notebook as much as she wanted, but she'd never understand the difference in texture, the . . . the skin of the dream itself that made divers' oneiric images so different from those of ordinary people. Marianne just dreamt, plain and simple, like everyone else, but David went elsewhere, slipped under the barbed wire of some mysterious border to enter a land known only to a privileged few.

"You're not listening to me," the psychologist observed. "David, you're wasting my time. I've been camped out here five days already, waiting for you to come out of your trance. If you think that's pleasant—"

"The job took a lot of prep," David pleaded. "Nadia had to figure out the jeweler's schedule so she could—"

"Christ! Are you doing this on purpose, or what? Is it some kind of provocation, is that it? Do you want to drive me crazy? Is that it? There was no 'job,' no 'jeweler'—that's all smoke and hot air, immaterial images."

David gave up arguing. Insisting would have been awkward; assistant psychologists were obsessed with schizophrenia. Their mouths were full of phrases like "loss of any notion of reality," "obsessive oneiric constructs." He had to avoid fanning the flames if he didn't want to end up in a clinic with an IV drip and electrodes all over his scalp.

"Just kidding," he apologized cautiously. Marianne glared at him, suspicious. She had a tomato sauce stain on the back of her lab coat. What had she been doing for five days, while he was drifting in a deep trance? He tried to picture her, tiptoeing in her careful, mousy way around the winding hallways of the large, awkwardly laid-out apartment passed down when his parents died. It was in an old building so damp the window frames were swollen shut. Carbon monoxide from the street had slowly upholstered the panes with a gray fluff that greedily filtered out the light. There reigned a shut-in smell, commingled with that of dust and stale frying oil; David had gotten used to it. The permanent gloom did not bother him, not in his line of work. He'd slathered everything in blue paint: the shelves of the massive library, the old upright piano, the Renaissance buffets, even the hallway flooring where a lack of rugs left the floorboards bare. The apartment as aquarium. Of course the rooms were weird, oddly-shaped, hard to furnish. Their too-high ceilings made them look a bit like corridors clumsily converted into lodgings, but it was his domain, and he loved it. For five days, Marianne had wandered through these rooms with her little pursed mouth. She'd deemed the decoration in bad taste, the books infantile. All those silly pulp magazines carefully slipcased with maniacal care, as if they were valuable!

More than anything else, David's library must have plunged Marianne into abysmal consternation for there, on overloaded, sagging shelves, he kept all the books and magazines he'd sated

himself on ever since he could read. The paperbacks were orga-
nized chronologically, not by date of publication, but by the date
David had first discovered them. A little label thumbtacked over
each row specified the age range its two feet of shelf covered:
8–10, 10–12 . . . At twelve, crime series began to appear, with
their violently gaudy covers, bare-shouldered women with out-
rageously slutty pouts, cigarette holder in one hand, revolver in
the other. Secret agents had replaced the musty gumshoes of romantic American noir. The first adventurers of the technological
era, they weren't so conceited as to fall back on their fists alone in
the face of every menace. Gadget men, the appliance salesmen of
intrigue, they traveled the world, their pockets, shoes, hats, and
ties jam-packed with felt-tip torpedo launchers, ballpoint blow-
torches, fountain pen transmitters . . . They kept poison in hollow
teeth, bombs in their fake heels, bazookas in their artificial limbs.
With them, it was deception through and through. A shoe-radio
gave them a direct line to the president of the United States, a
pair of x-ray glasses let them see through solid walls . . . David
had adored this fictional world, prodigious fodder for afterschool
daydreams. Those dog-eared little paperbacks whose cheap paper
went frightfully yellow the minute sun hit them—he had but to
brush them with a finger, and he saw himself at twelve again,
curled up on the living room rug behind the rampart of an armchair that insulated him from the real world, his sweaty hands
gripping the adventures of Agent BZ-00, aka The Liquidator, who
at this very second was leaving for Hong Kong in the company of
an Asian lady "too almond-eyed to be trustworthy." Despite the
years, the armchair hadn't budged from its spot. The part of the

rug unfurling in its shadow would forever be gummy with cookie crumbs caught in its weave, puddles of spilled soda. David cautiously avoided that corner of the room, and even made a strict point of not looking behind the seat. Something stopped him from doing so, a vague and magical anxiety, a fear—maybe the fear of suddenly being face-to-face with himself? Of finding a wizened little boy, a kind of doppelganger freed from the passing of time, who dwelled there still, a stowaway in his own life, furiously reading without a moment's rest.

Marianne must have drawn a thousand less than flattering conclusions from this stockpile of popular literature. What could she possibly know about the magic of those covers hacks had hastily daubed, using only crude colors squeezed right from the tube to portray women with bombshell breasts?

In the end, she'd probably told herself she was only rooting around for the good of her patient. To collect "material for interpretation." He could just picture her: breathlessly opening drawers, sweating with excitement under her gray wool. She'd plunge her hands with their bitten nails into packets of letters, seize upon photo albums. Research! Just a routine investigation, nothing personal about it.

Had she already gotten her hands on the spy cards twelve-year-old David had made with bits of cardboard snipped from shoeboxes? And the honor code, written in red ink, of the secret society founded the year he started sixth grade? The Club of the Scarlet Executioners . . . Three members, with their code names and passwords encrypted in a teacher-proof cipher. Yes, Marianne must have unearthed those quaint, poignant mementoes, those solemn licenses issued by some President of the Republic who wasn't good at spelling. And she hadn't been moved; her ugly little lips had vaguely pursed with scorn before such childishness. She'd simply thought how stupid little boys were at twelve when compared to girls, who . . .

And what about the graveyard of old toys? The former liquor cabinet he'd padlocked. But it was a dime store padlock, and Marianne probably had a whole ring of skeleton keys. They probably gave them out at the hospital: a burglary kit, lock picks an integral part of the paraphernalia, along with a stethoscope and the whole array of sedatives.

Every time he woke up, he found he hated the young woman a bit more, with her certainties and her bun. He was sure she never washed anything but her face and hands. She had a smell about her. A nasty little bitter sweat that stewed, muffled under her woolens. Where did she live when she wasn't squatting at her patients' apartments? Probably nowhere. She had no home of her own, a perpetual nomad, going from one building to another, camping out a week here, a few days there. She had nothing to her name but that well-worn, well-waxed suitcase. David pictured her sleeping inside it, pulling the top down over her head and sucking her thumb like a little old maid. In the end, they weren't so different from each other . . . and that was why he hated her.

He didn't like the idea of her sticking her nose into the graveyard of old toys, rifling through the rinky-dink odds and ends. Sheriff stars that twinkled no more, having lost their gilt. Pocketknives whose rusty, spring-loaded blades folded back into the handle only with a disillusioned squeal.

"You spat up blood again," she said, examining the inside of his mouth with a flashlight. "You'll need a fibroscopy."

"It happens a lot with mediums," objected David. "You know that. It just means the ectoplasm's texture is high quality, that's all."

Marianne shrugged and jotted something down quickly in her notebook. "Maybe you need to take a little break," she said. "You're too close to the dream world for my liking. You refuse to understand that Nadia is just a substitute for a maternal image. The words you use betray this obsession. Taking 'the plunge,' the undersea world where you become a kind of diver—how can you not read the classic elements of a fetal environment into all this? Your dreams reveal the desire for a typical intra-uterine regression. Learn to see them as just dreams, images projected by your subconscious that fade away the minute you open your eyes. Don't wind up one of those old dreamers who think the people in their dreams keep on living 'down below' while they're away, pining for them. Here, look what I found in your library."

She held up a much dog-eared spy novel from Alley Cat Books, on whose cover a young woman in a longshoreman's cap was springing from a long black car whose bodywork had something oily about it. *She's snooping! Snooping! She admits she's snooping!* David thought with vicious exultation, not even glancing at the illustration.

"C'mon," Marianne whined in a voice that annoyance made unpleasantly shrill. "Don't be a hypocrite. Look at that girl. She looks exactly like Nadia, the way you've described her. The cap, the red hair . . ."

"No way," David retorted. "Nadia's way cuter."

Marianne tossed the book disdainfully aside and got up, her cheeks red.

"Oh, you're becoming impossible to work with!" she screeched. "You think it's fun for me waiting around for you to wake up? This apartment is creepy! Those windows don't even open! All this blue, blue everywhere! I feel like I'm locked up in a drowned submarine! And why the soundproofing? You can't even hear noise from the street anymore. Sometimes I'd give anything in the world just to hear the neighbors' toilet flush! There's no TV, no radio—not even a real library, just these stupid books! Really, I—"

She ran from the room and locked herself in the bathroom. David didn't lift a finger to stop her. For a moment, he was tempted to take advantage of her absence and open the metal box at the foot of the bed, but gave up at the thought that she'd no doubt put a combination lock on it. "Down below" the lock would've been no match for his fingers, but up here he no longer benefited from the strange skills that faded from his brain as soon as he opened his eyes.

Marianne came back in. She'd run some water over her face.

"I'm ordering a full exam," she announced like a punishment. "Report to the medical center at the Fine Arts Academy tomorrow. It's long past time for a checkup. I'm not kidding. Put up a fight, and the museum will take disciplinary action. They may even revoke your art worker license."

She left the room without so much as a wave. David heard her buckle up her little suitcase, muttering incomprehensibly to herself. She appeared again, stuffed into an old blue coat, seized the metal box as if confiscating a toy from a child, and turned on her heel.

"I'll buy a radio!" David shouted just as she stepped out on the landing, "but only because you said so."

He lay back down again, unable to take his mind from the steel coffer Marianne was now hurrying to the storage center at the Museum of Modern Art. What had he created this time? Another knickknack? He was always bringing back novelties, curios for mantles or shelves. His works sat enthroned atop TVs, never in museums or the cellars of great collectors, bristling with alarms. His file described him as a "popular" sculptor, a "mainstream" artist. He didn't know if he should be worried or delighted. It was said that famous divers for wealthy art galleries suffered great agony; some even ended up dying from it.

He rose slowly and set his feet on the carpet with care. After a dive, the things up top, on the surface, seemed excessively, unbearably solid. The carpet stung the soles of his feet like sandpaper; his silk bathrobe weighed on his shoulders like a cement slab. Objects made war on him; everything was an assault. Even shaving cream chafed his cheeks. Down below, everything was so fluid, so supple . . . He hesitated before going into the bathroom. He was ready to bet the shower would be pure acid, and as for the food in the fridge—if there was any left—it'd be about as tasty as a shovelful of gravel flavored with tar. Better not to push it.

He dressed in slow motion, like a man fresh from an operation, afraid of splitting his sutures open with too brisk a movement. He felt weak. Five days of dieting. Marianne had hooked him up with a glucose drip, but that didn't fill your stomach. He decided to go down to the Divers' Café, an establishment strictly reserved for members of the profession, where you were weaned on milk and vanilla custard while waiting to reacclimate to the roughness of the real. It was a low room—a "colon," its detractors called it—bathed in a swimming pool's blue gloom, where everyone whispered without caring if anyone was listening. Monologues intertwined there, oneiric accounts endlessly rebegun, ecstatic descriptions, somnolent mumblings. It was like a sauna where you did your best to sweat out the last droplets of dream and readapt to normal life, an airlock that protected you for a little while longer from the dreadful confrontation with the light of day. No sooner were they torn from bed than divers hurried there, wrapped in thick woolens, eyes hidden behind huge sunglasses that turned them into groping blind men. They gorged themselves on milk and grenadine syrup, honey and cream, chocolate mousse, vanilla porridge . . .

David didn't really enjoy the company of other mediums. He'd soon realized that in such a confined setting there was no such thing as conversation; everyone soliloquized without paying any attention to what was going on around them, drunk on the sound of their own voices, sinking into self-hypnosis and narcissistic vertigo, endlessly recounting their last descent and the miracles they'd performed down below. He only ventured to the Divers' Café after coming back from a difficult expedition . . . and this one had been, no point lying about it anymore. Earlier, he'd been putting on a show for Marianne, but he couldn't fool himself: the job had gone wrong. Without Nadia's help, he'd have been stuck in the boutique, and the cops would've caught him red-handed. He felt a kind of fear, in retrospect, that made his stomach turn. He blamed himself for taking off too fast, ditching Nadia in the middle of the empty lot before he could see her get away with Jorgo, that kid with the smallpox-scarred face who knew everything there was to know about motorcycle acrobatics. What were they doing right now? Were they back at the hide-out, that old plastic doll factory they'd made their headquarters? Nadia would be smoking nervously, checking the sky in hopes of seeing David materialize. She'd light cigarette after cigarette. Later, she'd have bad breath and a pasty tongue. Jorgo would be tinkering with one of the twelve motorcycles cluttering the garage. He never stopped coming up with new kinds of fuel, devilish new compression systems . . . A good team, for sure. People he could count on. Friends like he'd never had on the surface. "When do you think he'll be back?" Nadia would ask for the tenth time. "It sounds so dangerous up there." And she'd lean out the window by the crate of grenades they kept there in case of a police raid.

"When you're done with your motorcycle," she told Jorgo, "take a look at the rabbet on the machine gun. It likes to jam."

"That's 'cause you hold the trigger down too long," grumbled the teen. "You have to fire in short, even bursts, or the metal gets hot and warps."

Yes, a good team, with a few nice jobs under their belt. Oh, far from notorious yet, but that would come; it was up to him, David, to give them the boost they needed, to tell them one day, "No more penny-ante stuff, we're going for the big score"—because that was how thieves had talked ever since he'd first watched police series on TV.

Dressed as if for winter, he paused at the door to his blue apartment. Did he really want to go out? Marianne had said there was nothing left in the fridge; now that he was back up, he had to start eating again. And shitting, and pissing . . . Funny, you never thought about stuff like that down there, and were no worse off for it, proof that all it took to get rid of bad habits was a little will-power. Or maybe it was because you had less time to get wrapped up in your own thoughts . . . to get bored. Up here, in the end, shitting and pissing passed the time. It was a kind of ceremony, a private little mass.

He went down the stairs, clutching to the banister with one hand. Yeah, he'd been showing off for Marianne. In fact, the job had been a really close one, and without Nadia . . . But no point bringing all that up with Marianne. Besides, she wasn't even a real psychologist, just some specialized nurse the Museum of Modern Art had recruited. She tried to pick up stuff from books, but she wasn't fooling anyone. She didn't believe, and never would. She could never understand how the plunge worked. "You talk about diving too much," she would say, "and not enough about coming back up, but that's the part the Museum's interested in. That's what you get royalties for. That's what allows you to 'bring' something back from the depths of sleep."

David shrugged and grimaced. He felt despondent; his joints ached. "From the pressure," he thought. "I should've made the decomp stops."

Outside, the street seemed appallingly noisy, crowded, and bright. It was an effort not to shrink back hurriedly under the awning.

[3]

The Next Day/
Visit to a Sad Zoo

Very early the next morning, he reported to the health clinic at the
Museum of Modern Art. It was easier for him to confront the outside world in the half-light of dawn, when the ink of night, barely
faded, still stained the streets and sky. He hugged the walls, leaping
from one pool of shadow to the next. Whenever he had to cross
a zone that was too brightly lit, he held his breath without even
thinking. The entrance to the clinic was at the rear of the building. The cellars and the former restoration studios had been re-
purposed to house works and their creators. It had required space,
and the daubs and sculptures of past masters had been dumped
on the market pell-mell. Junkmen and flea marketers had filed
through for weeks, carting away in ramshackle trucks canvases

by Picasso, Klee, and Hartung that had sold for a song. Who was still interested in a form of art now completely passé? Curators had been happy to see rag-and-bone men, with their own filthy hands, take down from the walls dusty paintings no one had come to gaze upon in forever. Even antique dealers no longer bothered to come when invited to a clearance sale, so utterly barbarous did they deem the old mediums of expression. "Paint applied to a piece of canvas with a stick topped by animal hair?" one of them had snickered at a cocktail party. "How crude! Why not excrement hand-smeared on animal hide?" David passed through security, flashing his art worker's card with the national flag, and threaded his way through the maze of damp corridors that led to the medical center. A sleepy doctor, cheeks blue-tinged with beard growth, put him through the usual tests while yawning, a cigarette damp with saliva stuck in a corner of his mouth. Once the last encephalogram had been recorded, David slipped out, making for the heart of the building. The corridors, with their narrow walls and terribly high ceilings, seemed to have been made for very tall, spindly creatures. *Depthless beings*, he thought. *Silhouettes able to slip through a mail slot.* He advanced down the hallway slowly, wondering if that was how the great painted figures of giant paintings once displayed in the main hall had fled. He had no trouble picturing the two-dimensional people detaching themselves from the paintings, stepping over the gilt frames and slipping away shamefully, head down, struggling against the occasional draft. That was how they had left for exile, for oblivion—through the artists' entrance at whose end awaited the terrible light of day. A light that would devour their colors once protected by carefully calibrated gloom. One after another, they had gone, as painting became an obsolete, piddling activity forgotten by the public. The landscapes, the coronations, the great battles, the depositions of Christ, the allegories had all emptied themselves of their subjects, their crowds, their nymphs. Only trees and objects had remained frozen on the canvas, too dumb to realize their hour of glory had passed. Or too prideful to consider it. Upon exiting the museum, the figures hadn't known what to do, had started walking in circles, giving way when shoved by a gust of wind. Those whose varnish was still intact had resisted the rain, while others had quickly begun to mold, to come undone. To withstand the wind that blew on the museum esplanade, they'd wound themselves round benches, great flapping oriflammes with knotted legs. The sun had gone to work on them then, bleaching colors, roasting varnish, hardening the fibers of old canvases. The faces of Madonnas, Christs, Generals of the Empire had slowly been erased; pink had turned gray, pigments exhausted by centuries of survival had faded. Eyes and mouths had grown progressively paler until there was nothing left in the forecourt but strips of white, vaguely anthropomorphic canvas which were mistaken for bits of tarp wind had torn from a scaffolding. Yes, that was how the museum's inhabitants had met their fate, the tenants of famous paintings, victims of a consumption to which no one had paid the slightest mind. David made his way forward step by step, like a burglar expecting at any minute to be pinned to the wall by a floodlight beam. He shivered at the slightest sound, an eye out for ghosts of the art of yesteryear.

Phantoms here didn't hide beneath bedsheets like their ancestors in Gothic novels, but beneath painted canvases. They slipped behind a crate, stole through tears in plastic sheeting to delude themselves that they were still hanging on the wall, the object of everyone's attention . . .

David shook himself to dispel the phantasmagoria assailing him. There were no ghosts, no straying images. If the frames were empty, it was because the paintings they once displayed had been relinquished to the naïve rapacity of junk dealers, nothing more.

He threw a quick look over his shoulder. He wasn't allowed in this part of the building. From here on out was the quarantined sector; only veterinarians were allowed to move around freely there.

At the end of the corridor, a fat man jammed into a less than immaculate lab coat kept watch from his perch on a stool. Arms crossed over his chest, he shifted from one butt cheek to the other, trying vainly to find a comfortable position. His red eyes bore witness to a desperate lack of sleep; all he wanted was to be in bed. David had been betting on the night shift's general fatigue. Relief was still an hour away, and a long night's duty had dulled their watchfulness. He had to take advantage of this slackened attention.

"Yeah," grumbled the man at the sight of a visitor suddenly emerging from the tunnel of the shadowy corridor. "What is it?"

David pulled a twenty from his pocket, rolled it up lengthwise, and, for kicks, began whistling through it as if it were a flute. The fat man watched him without any show of impatience.

THE DEEP SEA DIVER'S SYNDROME

"Yesterday," the younger man said at last. "Around eight. A girl from psych section, with a bun and a pinched-looking mouth?"

"Oh yeah," the fat man snickered. "Piehole? That's what we call her. She's no barrel of laughs. Probably frigid. That mouth isn't the only thing of hers that's pinched tight."

Grabbing the sign-in sheet, he ran a soiled finger down the columns. David flattened the twenty and slipped it in between the pages. "Yeah," said the man. "Just a quick look, though, or I won't hear the end of it. Dream Number 338. It was kinda weak; the doc on call put it in an incubator. You really want to see it?"

David tried on a pleading look. The watchman sighed, straightening up. "I just don't get it," he groused, "you guys're all the same. You sell 'em, and then you come down here crying for a look. Well, c'mon—I have to go with you. If we run into anyone, I'll say you're my brother-in-law."

He pulled an imposing key from his pocket and unlocked the great doors that led to the former exhibit halls. The windows had been blacked out, resulting in a gloom pierced by rays of sunlight where dense golden dust danced about. On pedestals that had once supported masterpieces of Greek art perched cages big and small. Simple wire affairs, or solid jails with bars. Right away, David recognized the smell of dreams, the "electric" smell of re-surfacing successfully.

"Those ones there are earmarked for auction," the watchman muttered. "They're fresh from quarantine. Got their photos taken for the catalog yesterday. One or two of 'em are gonna go for millions!" He kept waddling from one cage to the next, a nasty grimace on his face.

"I just don't get why you guys all want to look at them," he said again. "They've got no eyes, no mouth, nothing. *Scrambled eggs*, I call 'em—nice, right? There's a certain resemblance. Some of the other guys, they call 'em miscarriages, but that's not nice."

David hardly dared move. As with each time he managed to sneak into the storage room, he was struck with a mental and physical paralysis. "They're not even real animals," the fat man complained. "They don't piss, they don't shit. I was a watchman at the zoo for a while, I know what I'm talking about. These things, well, they look like they're alive, but no one's figured out just how that is. Man! I've fed lions and tigers; now, them you better not mess with. They'll gobble that meat on the end of your stick right up. But these things? Just what are they, anyway? They look like flesh, even skin, but at the same time, they're not part of our world. They've got no fur, no scales. You know, some of the guys even poke 'em to try to make 'em scream? But they never make a sound. What are they?"

"Dreams," David murmured. "Dreams, stolen from sleep."

"Stolen?" the big man grumbled. "I thought all this looked shady. Never thought I'd wind up guarding stolen objects!"

David wasn't listening to him anymore. He was like a kid on his first trip to the zoo, suddenly discovering that a rhinoceros wasn't just a funny-looking animal with a horn balanced on the end of its nose and leather chaps too big for its body, but a living, breathing thing, enormous and monstrously impossible. He didn't dare stick his hand through the bars of a big cage; the watchman probably would've stopped him anyway. But inside was something incredibly fragile, an organic . . . architecture? With skin more delicate than a petal. A kind of indefinable being, rolled up in a ball and barely touching the earth. Volumes harmoniously joined but lacking any precise vital function. This one looked like a shoulder. A giant shoulder so soft, so fragile, a mere brush of your finger would immediately mottle it with bruises. A belly? A breast, maybe. Or maybe all of the above at once, imbricate, interchangeable, but only just hinted at. As soon as you began walking around the cage, images poured forth, endlessly revising your first impression. No, it wasn't a breast, more a belly, the belly of a young girl . . . or a cheek, a cheek flushed pink by a spot of sun . . . No, no, it was a back. The marvelously smooth back of a woman bathing herself. It was . . . everything and nothing, all at once. Volumes whose fragility put a lump in your throat and halted you mid-gesture. An existential precariousness that made you an oafish brute, a bull in a china shop. A half-materialized sigh, still wavering between existence and dissolution. "Scrambled eggs," the watchman grumbled. "To think some people spend their whole lives gushing over these things!"

David shivered, uneasy. Though he still felt a visceral need to see the dreams he'd given birth to, upon seeing them he experienced nothing like the extraordinary rapture aesthetes spoke of.

"Well, of course," Marianne had told him bluntly. "Dreamers can't derive any pleasure from contemplating their dreams. You don't experience sexual arousal when you see your naked body in a mirror, do you? Well, same goes for the dreams you've materialized. Other people might derive a certain pleasure from them, but there'll always be something like an incest taboo between you and your own dream. Do you understand what I'm trying to say?" Yes, he understood: he was like those miners who dig gold from the depths of the earth for a large conglomerate. He labored, while others' hands fondled the ingots . . .

"Yours is a lot smaller," said the watchman, tugging David's sleeve. "Plus they're not done running tests on it yet. It might even die before it hits the market."

These words were uttered without a trace of meanness; he was just a man used to life's hard knocks. Giving David a shove as if they were old friends, he ushered him into a room filled with the hum of incubators. A greenhouse swelter reigned; sweat sprang to their brows. Just like everywhere else, lighting was reduced to a strict minimum, and it was hard to get an exact idea of just what was being stored in the incubators. The fat man checked a chart and tried to orient himself among the rows.

"Over there," he whispered. "The vet isn't done vaccinating it yet."

David leaned toward the bell jar, ringed in a halo of moisture. For most dreams, the mandatory quarantine was a terrible ordeal. Many of them couldn't stand up to the numerous injections and samplings the boy butchers at the lab believed it their duty to inflict.

"You never can tell," Marianne would utter with an erudite air whenever David let his indignation show. "Dreams come straight from sleep, so they could be vectors for sleeping sickness.

A few troubling cases of a slowdown in bodily functions have been recorded among collectors who spend lots of time contemplating their acquisitions. Yes, in some cases even trance state and memory loss. Dreams aren't as harmless as you claim. We must be very cautious." Being cautious meant pricking that wondrous skin with long needles, slicing into it with scalpels, scarifying these organisms until they finally shriveled up and disintegrated. "If they croak before making it out the laboratory door," asked the watchman, "do you still get paid?"

"You get a kill fee," David replied mechanically. "It's not much, but enough to carry you till the next dive."

"And if it goes to auction?"

"Ten percent of the selling price."

The fat man frowned and leaned over the incubator. "It's not very big," he observed. "That's not gonna make you rich. Strictly for small savers. My sister-in-law, owns a deli? She loves these things. Her mantle's covered in 'em."

David blinked, but the condensation inside the bell jar kept him from clearly making out the contours of the dream. He recalled the two bags of uncut gems he'd taken from the safe in the jewelry shop down below, and the crunch of raw diamonds against his chest . . . that had been the symbolic image allowing the dreamer's attractional energies to be concentrated. A sort of fictional target you focused on before casting your net. Deep in the incubator was something pink and plump, with soft, gentle curves. A little netsuke, perhaps, a blissful and mysterious sphere that emanated a kind of harmonious satisfaction, a soothing radiation. No, that wasn't it at all, it was . . . oh, what was the use? No one ever managed to describe the oneiric ectoplasms, anyway. No two people ever saw them the same way. A round and stretchy Buddha? A hairless cat, sleeping in a ball, a—damn it! Did he have to go seeing some kind of link between its morphology and the symbolic image of bags snatched from a safe? Psychologists rejected any connection, but psychologists reasoned according to theories, clinical reports. Not one of them was capable of diving into the depths of sleep and bringing back something solid, something . . . alive. Not one of them had the *power*, and that very thing made them hostile, that impotent jealousy.

"C'mon, move along," the watchman ordered. "Can't loiter around here or you'll get caught. You've seen it now, so, what? Feel better? It's not like it's a baby, right? Hey, you look like a first-time dad who's just gotten a secret glimpse of his kid behind his wife's back. Weird, isn't it? You mediums, you're not quite normal. But then you never claimed to be!"

David didn't claim a thing. He thought about the little dream imprisoned in its incubator. "Don't say *dream*," Marianne said whenever he used the word. "It's an incorrect and stupidly sentimental term. It's not a dream, it's an ectoplasmic product a sleeping medium has materialized from an oneiric image haunting his brain. The dream allowed you to create this *object* by stimulating your imagination—that's all." Was that really all there was to it? David didn't believe it for a second. These *objects* were cut from the very skin of dreams; for him, they were proof that down below a woman's flesh was softer than anywhere else. A woman's flesh . . . Nadia's. Especially Nadia's.

"Don't come 'round here again for a while, OK?" the fat man whispered to David as he escorted him out. "I don't think this is good for you. Tell yourself it's like a deformed kid you were forced to leave at child services. Better that way in the end, right?"

[4]

Afternoon/A Walk in an Antiseptic Desert

Upon leaving the museum, David realized that it was Sunday, a day he'd long associated in his mind with activities like ritual visits to cemeteries, hospitals, or public parks full of retirees taking in the sun. When he was ten or so, he'd decreed one fine morning that in coded language the word Sunday meant "the day of the dead," because the empty streets seemed to bear witness to a sudden embolism in the city, shops stood padlocked behind metal shutters, and the rare survivor you ran into here and there had the gait of a convalescent, quite unlike the weekday pace that sent people charging toward subway entrances as if an air-raid siren had just urged them toward shelter in rail tunnels. David hated Sunday, a day of anemic languor when the streets seemed suddenly to be short of blood, only the odd car circulating, or, worse yet, bicycles.

He wandered across the esplanade. Luckily it wasn't very nice out, and the city was still enveloped in a vague fog that made its hard angles bearable. He decided to walk to the clinic that cared for dreamers with work-related injuries. The establishment was on the other side of the bridge, in the compound of the former marble depot where sculptors once came looking for raw material for their work: stone slabs hewn from state quarries. The main room on the ground floor had been summarily converted, divided with folding screens and curtains on great sliding tracks as in a medieval hospice. Meant as a "temporary" setup, it had dragged on for several years already. At the Ministry of Cultural Affairs, no one really cared about broken-down divers whose strange afflictions were the despair of the medical profession and profoundly annoyed doctors.

David crossed the bridge and had lunch in a bistro cramped as a concierge's quarters, where a fat man was cooking up an enormous pot of onion soup on a little hot plate. He tried not to think too much about the veterinary quarantine room and his dream, imprisoned in its muggy incubator. He wondered if he could maybe grease the watchman's palm and get him to personally oversee the growth of that overly fragile little thing slowly coming into its own under its bell jar. Couldn't it be spared a few tests if its charts were hidden, or even tampered with? Sure, it'd cost a lot of money, but David told himself that was the price of making sure his work survived. His last few dreams had died in quarantine, poisoned by ham-fisted vets who thought they were still working on plow horses and jabbed at dreams as if inoculating hippopotami.

He lapped up his soup, brooding over the idea, downed two cups of very sweet black coffee, and headed out toward the marble depot. The compound's great courtyard was still littered with useless chunks no one would ever come for now, and these rain-soiled slabs had ended up forming a kind of miniature mountain range firmly rooted in the muddy ground. Just past the main gates, you found yourself deep in a labyrinth of abandoned megaliths richly slathered in pigeon shit. It was like a garden of stone, a pagan cathedral of menhirs raised to the sky. The ruins of some unknown disaster lost to memory. Wandering among these forgotten monoliths, David wound up convinced he was crossing the wreckage of a bombed-out city reduced to its bare foundations. He found the sheer enormity of the slabs somewhat frightening, and hastened his step toward the far side to exit the oppressive enclave.

Upon entering the building, he flashed his card at a sullen orderly who waved him along, stifling a yawn. "I'm here to see Soler Mahus," David explained. "They haven't moved him?"

The orderly rolled his eyes as if he'd just been asked a particularly moronic question, and dove back into reading his paper. David hesitated at the room's threshold; on the heels of the stone labyrinth was now one of curtains shivering in the drafts. It was as if they'd hung a gargantuan load of laundry out to dry . . . or the sails of a ship. David ran his gaze over the canvas expanse, trying to pick out a mizzen, a jib . . . He gave himself a shake. They weren't sails, just rough, thick curtains. Numbers had been painted on them to help you find your way around. When would he get over the annoying foible of always seeing things in other things?

Once a week, he came to see Soler Mahus, an old diver who'd

suffered a serious decompression accident. Soler's brain was deteriorating as the months went by. He had gone prematurely gray, and the prolonged bed rest had melted his muscles away, reducing his body to a skeletal schematic wrapped up in cellophane skin that would tear at the slightest scratch. David had nothing to say to him, but Soler liked to soliloquize before a willing audience. The accident had stripped him of his powers, and he no longer lifted a finger to fight his illness. The doctors paid him erratic visits, not knowing what cure to prescribe, content to cram him full of sedatives while waiting for his EEG to flatline.

David went up the central aisle. The worn, porous stone had been sprayed down with some milky disinfectant still stagnating in the cracks between slabs. After getting it wrong twice, he finally found Soler's cell and pulled back the curtain. The old man didn't move a muscle, didn't even wink to greet his guest. For two months now, his facial muscles had been almost completely paralyzed, and he spoke in a curious ventriloquist's voice, without moving his lips. No sooner was David was seated at his bedside than he resumed his monologue, as if the young man had simply slipped away for a moment. Maybe he didn't notice the passing of time, and believed his visitor had just returned from the bathroom?

"Did I ever tell you about my Bengal safari?" he murmured, his face not betraying the slightest expression. "It was Prince Rajapur who had summoned me. Twelve elephants, a veritable army of beaters. The tiger was a great male, a child-eater ravaging the villages of the region. They'd been trying to corner him for a year now, but he was a sly beast, extraordinarily cunning, orange as flame, with stripes of camouflage that made him almost invisible to the naked eye. But his breath was atrocious, and . . ."

David wasn't really listening. Soler's imaginarium didn't really overlap with his own fantasies, but he knew that every dreamer haunted his own territory. In his youth, Soler Mahus had been weaned on tales of adventure and big game hunting. He too had once owned a library full of twopenny pulps. From these storybook memories, he'd built a world made of jungles and vast rivers cleaving sunburnt lands in two, savannahs, all-devouring deserts, through which he tracked fantastical beasts, legendary animals whose atrocities local tribes recounted in fearful whispers. Mahus hunted down the white rhino, the white gorilla, the white tiger . . . ghostly creatures, each the only living one of its kind. Wild monsters whose white coats contrasted strangely with green forests thick with sap. *Down below*, he'd been a great hunter bristling with bullets, sporting an anaconda-skin hat. A formidable stalker of the savannah who made his own cartridges, whose catchphrase—no matter the adversary—was always "Boys, don't shoot till you see the whites of their eyes!" He'd faced down the fiercest predators, felled at point-blank range elephants driven mad by a poisoned assegai. He'd had every tropical disease there was, every fever, every pox. He'd eaten quinine by the fistful, sewn his wounds shut with his own two hands. His body (his body down there) was but a quilt of scars, an appallingly stitched figure no white woman could gaze upon without immediately hiding her eyes. The negresses were the only ones to lick his wounds, and they did so with the tips of their tongues, naming him a great warrior, knowing what they gazed on was indomitable courage.

But Soler cared little for women. He came and went, content with a virgin offered up by some unworthy kinglet during a quick halt; then once more he was the ascetic hunter of endless expeditions. The mad monk whose rifle was loaded with bullets he'd carved Xs into. He sought the white beast, the one he had to kill at any price and throw over his shoulder if he wanted to go back up with a trophy . . .

"Did I ever tell you the one about the lion of Magombo? Or the panther of Fijaya?" His monologues always started out the same way. He never bothered waiting for an answer, and dove right into an endless, convoluted tale, full of backtracking and contradictions. He'd once successfully hunted down a tiger in Africa—it hadn't posed him the slightest problem of believability.

"Or the Raja of Shaka-Kandarek's safari? And the great massacre of the mad gorillas? And the tale of the leopard with the golden claws?" Stories, so many stories. Down below, he was Majo-Monko, He-Who-Slew-Like-Lightning. He had his friends, his chief spear-carrier: Nemayo, a prince of the savannah, sole survivor of a tribe wiped out by a terrible civil war. Nemayo, an athlete slender as an assegai, his face covered in ritual scars and his body in inscrutable tattoos. Nemayo knew the lair of every legendary beast, was never scared of any taboo; he alone remained, faithful, when the whole troop of porters had scattered in the jungle at the first roar.

"Kid," Soler whispered. "I was happy down there. I hunted the great white beasts. It was hard—terrible, sometimes—but that's life, real life! Know what I'm saying?"

David understood. For a long time, Soler had worked as a packer in the basement of a department store, hiding his power for fear of being persecuted. Changing fashions had delivered him from this hell, making him a star overnight. The great white beasts . . . how many had he killed? Monstrous gorillas, taller than trees, which once brought to the surface had become magnificent works of art. Oneiric ectoplasms (as the psychologists would say) of sufficient size to be displayed in public spaces. For Soler dreamed grandly, majestically. For ten years, he'd been the toast of every museum and collector. His dreams were too meaty, too robust to have anything to fear from being put through quarantine. At the mere mention of his name, auction prices shot through the roof, buyers went into a frenzy.

"I was so bored up here," he kept saying, "up top everything was ugly, just horrible. My real life was down below. You're like me, you know what I'm saying. Plus whenever I stayed up top for too long, things would start to go bad in my own personal Africa, the tribes would start fighting, poachers would go around slaughtering game with machine guns. Nemayo would say, 'You must not go, bwana. No sooner do you leave for the surface than misfortune falls upon us, all goes wrong, epidemics ravage the savannah.' Plus it killed me not to know how they were doing. You feel that way too, right? The sudden desire to ring them up on the phone. Sometimes I'd open my mailbox automatically, hoping to find a muddy, dirty, wrinkled envelope inside with an African stamp on it. But there was never anything. They can't write to us. That's the hardest part: exile. My health got worse, the doctors wanted to keep me from diving. They said, 'You're staying too long down there, Mr. Mahus. It's bad for your brain. You have to limit your forays into dreams, your last scan wasn't very good, there were shadows . . .' I didn't give a damn about their shadows. I told them, 'But it all goes to hell down there as soon as I turn my back! It's obvious you don't know the colonies! There's this tribe, the Mongo-Mongos, cannibals who come down from the mountains and snatch children away because they're tenderer than animals. Everyone's afraid of them except for me, me and Nemayo. But Nemayo won't do anything if I'm not there, those great stoic savages can be so abominably fatalistic!' My words fell on deaf ears. They gave me drugs that kept me from dreaming. Stuff that fills your brains with lead, cement, that sends you tumbling into a barren sleep, imageless, the sleep of plants . . . Yeah, that's probably how salads sleep, and cabbages too. And potatoes. The sleep of morons! Don't ever let them drug you, kid! Ever! Even if they say you're sick, even if they say you've got deep-sea diver's syndrome. That's what they call the jones to go back down. They claim divers who're hooked really just want to go to sleep down there and never come back up. Bullshit. They're just jealous."

Sometimes he would stop to rest his throat muscles. At such moments, he looked like he'd fallen asleep, vanquished by exhaustion, but soon he'd start talking again, cursing doctors and psychologists.

"Drugs are poison. When I dove again, after a year's rest, I was terrified by what I found waiting for me down below. The drugs had poisoned the rivers and the trees. The animals had died.

Deep in the heart of Pandaya, crocodiles were floating belly-up downstream. Even the vultures wouldn't eat the rotting hippo carcasses. The whole jungle was festering, polluted by sedatives. It pained me to see what had happened to Nemayo. I found him sitting atop a hill. When I tried to walk up, he cast stones at me. He had leprosy—the tranquilizers had made him a leper. He'd eaten of the moldering flesh of the dream, and he himself had begun rotting too. He wept, hiding his mutilated face beneath a zebra hide. 'The white beasts were the first to die,' he sobbed, 'and their cadavers infected the entire jungle. The earth began to decompose. You were gone too long. You should have come back, bwana. As soon as you left we grew weak, our bodies became feeble, unable to fight off illness. We were overcome with dejection, and weariness. We remained inert, sprawled on the ground, staring at the sky, hoping to catch a glimpse of you. Men no longer made love to their women, and predators lost their appetite for their prey, and the grass no longer had the strength to grow, and the fruits were without flesh or flavor. It is you who give us the will to live, you alone. Why did you stay up there so long, on the surface? Is the tobacco there more flavorful? Are the women they give you more beautiful? Do they save you better parts of the hunt?' He was a savage, kid, but it pained me to see him in such distress. I told him, 'I'm here to stay, Nemayo, and you'll heal, the earth will heal, and all will be as it was before,' but he just kept weeping. He said, 'It's too late, all the great white beasts are dead, woe is upon us, and even the girls are no longer born virgins.'"

"I struck out deep into the jungle with my faithful over-under

Gambler-Wimbley, my bandoliers full of bullets, and enough food for a week, but he was right, the great white beasts were dead, and their corpses were sinking into the earth like rotten aspic. A gooey snow—can you picture that? Snow like runny marshmallows. That's all that was left of the mythical creatures. Right then I got so scared that the nightmare tore me from my dream and I shot right up, straight past all the decompression stops. I thought my head and my lungs were about to explode. I tried hard to hang on anything I could—trees, rocky outcrops—but the nightmare had done its job, forcing me back up. I hit the surface screaming.

"At the hospital, they told me I had an effusion in one of my cervical lobes, a blood vessel had burst. I shouted, 'It's because I came back up too fast,' and they said, 'It's from overwork.' Not long after that, my brain started hardening. I know it's because of the drugs, the medicine. The dead dreams are drying out, setting inside my head. The dead bodies of Nemayo and everyone else have ossified my brains. They're in there, I can feel them. They just keep getting heavier, pulling the nape of my neck into the depths of my pillow. It's no tumor, it's a whole dead world, a jungle with its animals and tribes. It's everything from below in necrosis, with its rivers poisoned by tranquilizers. Don't ever let them treat you, ever. If they give you drugs, spit 'em out. They claim they're trying to help us, but actually they're waging war on our people, our worlds. A dirty war whose damages you won't even see right away. If you've got people down below who are dear to you, protect them. Don't make the same dumb mistake I did."

Every time Soler fell silent, David couldn't help looking at the sick man's head sunken deeply in the pillow. It was said that the brains of divers with the bends slowly calcified, taking on a porcelain aspect. One day Marianne had insisted on showing David a pathological brain sample floating in a jar to persuade him of the realities of the risks he was running by stubbornly attaching too much importance to the dream world.

"Looks like a piece of a soup dish," he'd snickered, trying to stay composed, but the brittle brain hitting the sides of the jar with a sound like rattling plates had terrified him.

"They should've written me," Soler was mumbling, "they should've warned me about what was going on down there. But Nemayo didn't know the language of white men. Maybe he tried calling me with the tam-tam? I must have mistaken the beating of my heart for the pounding of jungle drums. Oh, I should've paid more attention! That's the terrible part: this exile. The impossibility of holding even a semblance of conversation . . ."

Slowly, David rose to his feet. A nurse had just drawn back the curtain and signaled that it was time for Soler's treatment. What kind of treatment did you give a man whose brain was turning to porcelain?

David slipped quietly away without so much as a goodbye from Soler. "And now I can't go back down there anymore," the old man had once told him. "When I try to dive, all I can see is a bottomless black hole, which frightens me. Then I get vertigo, and I stay sitting on the edge of my springboard, here in reality."

David left the marble warehouse, staring at the tips of his

shoes so as not to see the bogged-down slabs. Back home, he checked his mailbox automatically, to make sure Nadia hadn't written him. He shut the mailbox immediately, thinking, *That was stupid.*

Yes, stupid . . . but he hadn't been able to help himself.

[5]

The . . . Days? That Follow/ The Flour of Dreams

He had to eat. In the kitchen, the big fridge plundered by Marianne's passing gaped wide like an empty wardrobe. David, who filled it whenever the young woman was to assist him on a dive, remained dumbfounded by the psychologist's astounding appetite. How did a body that severe, whose veins and tendons traced branchings a blind man could've read with his finger like a page from an anatomy text in braille, manage to wolf down so much food without putting on an ounce of fat? For David was sure that naked, Marianne would offer up the spectacle of a nun smugly steeped in her own deprivations. A hard flesh, stripped to the bare minimum, a machine flesh designed to ensure precision work. As for David—stark muscles tautly rolled around rods of bone, all wrapped up in the tightest-fitting skin, a skimpy suit from a close-fisted tailor cutting costs and corners—he distrusted cadaverous foods. Red meat, fish, the sallow flesh of fowl gave him the creeps. Usually, he lived on buttered bread and coffee with milk. He'd stuffed his cupboards to bursting with bags of coffee, a phenomenal array in flavors harsh and delicate. In the fridge, he kept a slab of butter as yellow as ancient gold, from which he detached fine shavings by means of an iron cable strung between two sticks of wood. He sat down to eat as if to a ritual, picking up a great big plate—thick and heavy, its enamel cracked. His greatest delight consisted of slicing the bread with a knife sharper than a razor blade. He liked watching the bread fall, hearing the crust crunch and crackle. First the knife would labor at that browned hide, then the barrier gave way and the blade plunged into the divine marrow of the close, springy crumb. Serious as any specialist, he required bread that was dense as a sponge, able to sop up great quantities of liquid. More than anything, he hated bread that was full of holes, overtormented by yeastly effervescence. At the first hint of moisture such bread fell to shreds, failed to hold together in the mouth. Two quick bites and it came apart, obliterated when the pleasure was just beginning. High priest of breakfast, David conducted a ritual at once epicurean and austere, banishing jam, croissants, and even brioche, which for him represented an extremity of depraved sybaritic decadence. For a while he'd tried making his own bread, obeying some strange inner stubbornness to live off the grid, depending as little as possible on others. Fermenting yeast had given him too much trouble, and he'd been forced to give up. At first it had upset him, since he had a hard time finding a bakery with bread that met his standards. People today were fine with any old subpar product, and the bakehouses of yore had become automated factories where an artisan's barely flour-dusted hand was reduced to pushing buttons. David had wandered from bakery to bakery, sullen, despairing of ever finding the spongy bread that was his one and only fare, when he'd met Madame Antonine.

Antonine was plump and pink. A butcher, you'd have thought, raised on glazed ham, but her being a baker led you to liken her skin to the marzipan of her cakes. Antonine reigned over a bakery of blue and gold that the hot breath of ovens filled with the aroma of leavener. She was a widow. A little widow with the shoulders of a wrestler who'd left the ring and let her muscles be sweetly sheathed in fat. Right from the start David had pictured her bare-knuckled, battling the raw, rebellious, clingy dough. He knew kneading called for a great deal of physical strength and quickly gave you arms of steel. Antonine was a warrior princess of the ovens who'd let herself get a little chubby, so as not to frighten customers. She wore her potbelly as a polite disguise, but one punch from her could've laid out a junkyard mutt. Her apprentices feared her, and it was said she never thought twice about raising a hand to the pastry chef. When her authority was questioned, she drew herself to her full, fearsome height over the mixer tub, her face white with flour, and sent a ball of raw, gummy dough hurtling right between your eyes, knocking you breathless and almost smothering you. Antonine smelled like flour, David had noticed the first time she'd led him into her bed. As if her body were powdered head to toe and slid beneath your fingertips, almost silky, talcumed. She could've crushed David in her wrestler's arms, but she let him do as he wished, going with the flow, let herself be docilely manhandled.

"I want you to knead me," she said. "Go ahead. Use your fingers."

David obeyed, seizing her great white breasts, her thick belly, with delectation. He worked her as if she'd change shape when it was all over, be reborn in another form. Antonine had blonde hair and milky skin. Out of some inexplicable vanity, she shaved her pubic hair. She shared her lover's passion for breakfast. Like him, she hated cakes, creams, icings, candied fruit, preferring instead the austere nobility of peasant bread and butter with sea salt. In the tiny apartment above the bakery she made coffee the old-fashioned way, her mother's way.

"Filtered through a sock," she said, astoundingly strong, two cups knocked you flat on your back in bed, heart hammering in your chest.

"You're my artist," she cooed at him inanely, slicing thick hunks from the bread she'd made especially for David. He liked making love to her above the sweltering bakery, in the smell of fresh batches, when warmth exalted the fragrance of yeast, blending it with that of the baker's cunt.

"I'm the only one who knows how to make the bread you love," she murmured to him. "Without me, you'd starve to death." She was right, in a way; apart from his unending breakfasts, all David managed to choke down was a few spoonfuls of soup.

"Out in the country, soup is a part of breakfast," Antonine assured him, trying to prove that accepting this substance was in no way a breach of his strange code. She loved feeding him in bed, patting his cheeks, settling the great tray of unfinished wood over his knees. Then she would sit at the foot of the bed and butter the slices almost devoutly, a pudgy geisha with astonishingly graceful gestures. David stuffed himself, sinking his teeth into the chewy inside, glutted with café au lait. Then they would make love again, among the crumbs, and Antonine climaxed with a graceful little yelp, for this woman, with her lavish body, was discreet indeed in expressing her pleasure. She yipped, nose buried in David's shoulder, kneading the woolen mattress with her stubby fingers. A castaway washed up on his mistress's belly, David would fall into a light sleep while heat from the ovens erupting below came up through the floorboards, threatening to bake them both where they lay.

When she wasn't busy selling bread, Antonine collected dreams. David had come upon this passion the first time she'd had him up to her apartment. On the mantle in the narrow living room he'd suddenly spotted one of his most recent works. A dream of middling size that had met with critical success at auction. Antonine was an avid collector; as soon as an exhibit was announced, she ordered the catalog and spent hours engrossed in the contemplation of the works on offer. This taste for art kept her from saving up any money, but she made no complaint. That first night, taking David by the hand, she'd led him through every room, showing him the dreams heaped on shelves and hutches like tchotchkes. The ectoplasms, each on their numbered pedestal as required by law, looked somewhat sappy amid her furnishings, a flowering of lace, placemats, and pink lampshades with pom-poms.

"This one's yours too!" Antonine trumpeted, twirling around.

"And this one!" David was embarrassed. For a moment he felt like a prodigal husband watching his wife parade before him a string of children he was no longer able to recognize as really his own.

"This one's yours." Yes—it was like she was picking and choosing from a litter. "This one's yours, but that one's from the postman . . ." She flaunted her infidelities with a tiny apologetic smile.

"See," she murmured at the end of the tour, "you could almost say I'm a fan." David stammered something incomprehensible. He could recall with perfect clarity the circumstances surrounding the capture of each and every dream on display. The one over there on the mantle, by the little porcelain shepherdess mollycoddling a sheep in a pink bow—now that had been hard-won. Nadia had been wounded in the thigh by a guard who'd come charging from the back of the shop, and David had had to carry her on his shoulders while Jorgo covered their retreat, showering the front window with buckshot. Yes, the horrific din of explosions still rocked his ears. He saw the great yellow cartridges the breech-block ejected bouncing off the body of the car. And that other one over there, nestled by a seashell-covered box some laborious brush had inscribed with the legend *Souvenir de Sainte-Amine . . .* he'd had to extract that one from a booby-trapped safe that spat gouts of acid. The image of Nadia's jacket sizzling at the bite of the corrosive liquid had stayed with him . . .

"I don't keep track of how much I spend," Antonine explained. "At first, I was scared to raise my hand at the auctions. I felt like everyone was looking at me. Now I don't think twice.

I feel so good now that they're there on my shelves, like little soldiers watching over me. I can't tell you, the nightmares I used to have, the insomnia, how often I woke up screaming. And the knot here, between my breasts, like a fist squeezing the breath out of me. No matter what I did, I couldn't get any sleep, couldn't have nice dreams anymore, like I had when I was a girl. I was even afraid of going to bed at night. I'd pace around the bed, inventing a thousand excuses to postpone ever having to slip between the sheets."

She told him about the death of her husband, the baker, which had terrified her so. The victim of a stroke, he'd fallen face first into a tub of dough, and it had suffocated him. They'd never really managed to clean it all off afterwards, and he had to be buried that way, eyebrows and mustache thick with dough. It made him look like a clown who'd done a bad job taking off his makeup. Antonina hadn't cried too much; he was an old man with bad kidneys who'd asked her to marry him when she was going through a rough patch—in fact, she'd just broken her wrist during a wrestling bout, and . . . Two weeks after the funeral she began to be plagued by horrible nightmares. She would see a big fat boule on the table. A huge, fat boule of bread making a curious nibbling noise. When, after lengthy hesitation, she'd cut it in two, she found the head of her late husband inside, busily devouring the crumb. Then she'd wake up screaming, and stay sitting upright all night long, unable to sleep.

The situation couldn't go on without hurting her business. Wary at first, she bought a dream on a neighbor's advice. It was a handsome object, a trifle of a bauble, on a pretty pedestal . . . but what was it supposed to mean? The abstract aspect of the work had troubled Antonine, embarrassed her a bit. She only liked things you didn't have to go to school to appreciate. Real art—not excuses for intellectual jerking off that sent rich people into ecstasies. She'd dithered in the shop, turning the knickknack over and over in her fleshy hands.

"You're not supposed to touch them too much," the man in the shop had explained, making a face. "It shortens their lifespan." So they were expensive, *and* fragile? That had given her pause.

"Just do it," her neighbor had whispered, nudging her with an elbow. "It'll do you a world of good. I used to be just like you. Now I spend my whole pension on this stuff, but no more nightmares, no more sleeping pills, no more sedatives. I sleep like a baby, twelve hours a night! A woman of my age—can you imagine? My aches and pains no longer wake me, I lie down and just melt away, like a sugar cube. And it's all thanks to dreams. You dissolve, your body disappears, your brain dozes off—it's bliss. Saints and real nuns—the ones from the old days—must've felt something like it."

Antonine had left herself be swayed. In women's magazines, dreams were spoken of as wonderful mood stabilizers. "With just a few ectoplasmic curios carefully placed around your bedroom, you'll enjoy a veritable rejuvenating experience in the comfort of your own home. Your body will flourish, your skin will grow softer, *your wrinkles will disappear!*" Everyone sang the benefits of dreams, and declared that there was no longer any need to buy costly works of art to see your life transformed. To sleep like a baby . . . it was all she asked. Being rid of those horrible nightmares, that head she found every night in boules of bread, its mouth stuffed with crumb—aah! If this kept up she'd lose her health. She'd already lost weight, and didn't feel like doing anything anymore, not even making love, whereas once . . .

She would've liked it better if the knickknack was an actual art object—a little marquise, for instance. She didn't really like Greek statues, with their weenies and fig leaves. Fig leaves were stupid, and besides, how did they stay up? Was there a string? A spot of glue? Weenies were cute, especially in marble, all pink like a snail without a shell. Dreams were something else altogether. You weren't sure which angle to look at them from. They had no front or back, and everyone saw whatever they wanted to see: a child's head, a flower, a smiling cloud. In the end, she bought the object.

"Is Madame thinking of starting a collection?" the man in the shop had inquired. "If so, there are rules."

She'd had to learn the rules. Above all, never touch or caress the dreams, even if you got a sudden urge to, for human contact shortened their lifespans, and they withered faster. Naïvely, she'd asked how such a phenomenon manifested itself, and the man in the shop had lowered his voice to whisper evasively: "Oh, you know, they're kind of like flowers. Harmless. Just be sure to read the instructions." She'd brought the tchotchke home and set it on the mantle in her little bedroom. That night, she decided to leave the light on so she could keep an eye on it. She couldn't really see anything specific in it. A bird? A fat sleepy pigeon?

For the first time since her husband's death, she slept like a baby. A slumber like a long downy crossing, without a single image, without any of the absurd adventures that assail you as soon as you close your eyes. When she woke, she felt comfortable in her own skin, felt hungry for a huge breakfast, felt like running down to the bakehouse to knead dough and browbeat the apprentices. She was bubbling over with barely contained energy. From that day on, she began to collect dreams, haunting auction halls when she had enough money, and when she didn't, making do with little "art boutiques" or even the home décor sections of larger department stores.

"Haven't you ever wanted to buy a Soler Mahus?" David would ask. "You've seen the one at the Museum of Modern Art, right? The big dream in the rotunda?"

"Oh, no," she would protest. Soler Mahus was too pretentious, too monumental, it was impressive and even a bit intimidating. She only liked little things—fragile, delicate things, like the ones David made. "Nothing in the world could make me want a Soler Mahus," she decreed, mussing the young man's hair, "but on the other hand, I sure do love your little gumdrops. They're real, they're cute, they don't take up too much space, and they last long enough. You're not that sad when they wither away, because you're already tired of them."

David forced a smile. Antonine was a good girl. For her, there was no work of art as good as a big warm loaf of bread, and maybe she was right. She was completely unaware of upsetting her lover when she saddled his dreams with the nickname Gumdrops. In David, she saw a kind of homegrown faith healer, "with the gift but not the craft." She appreciated dreams for their therapeutic qualities, not for their intrinsic beauty. She even grew downright incredulous when told certain connoisseurs kept their collections locked up in rooms wired with alarms. For Antonine, dreams were like flowers: they made life more pleasant, and when they withered, well, you went and bought more.

She slept like a baby, her wrinkles faded away, her knees creaked no more . . . and best of all, dark thoughts no longer plagued her like before: insidious ailments that took root in the belly unawares, wars, attacks. The fear of being assaulted at night in the bakery. All those shadows had evaporated. Now all she had to do was lie down in bed and dissolve like a sugar cube. Sometimes she even wanted to reach out and stroke one of the tchotchkes.

"It's like dough," she would murmur when trying to explain these urges. "But magic dough, unreal. A terribly light, almost glowing dough. For making communion wafers, maybe? You know what I mean?" In such moments of ecstasy she placed her fingers on the object's surface but drew them back almost immediately, "because it felt alive." Lukewarm and yielding, too, like skin—not at all like a statuette of marble or ivory. It was an object and almost an animal at the same time.

"It's the skin of dreams," David explained. "That's why no one ever gets tired of looking at them."

"And that's what you make, sweetie pie," she said, imprisoning him in her great arms. "In the end, you're kind of a magician."

A magician? No—a medium, maybe even an artist. But David had no desire to go into any long explanations. He ate Antonine's bread and made love to her. That was how he got by between dives, willing prisoner of an eternal breakfast.

[6]

A Day Without Mail

The hardest part of being between dives was the blind, deaf wait that the mutual impermeability of the two worlds imposed. Like any diver, David dreaded these derelict stretches that made him shrivel into the hollow of an armchair, one eye glued to the phone. He couldn't keep from hoping for a call, a letter. Sometimes, when he couldn't take it anymore, he'd run down the stairs four at a time to the lobby and check his mailbox. What was he expecting? A damp letter from below? A message from Nadia in a bottle? Every time he opened the little metal locker he expected to smell silt, stick his hand in a tangle of seaweed, but nothing ever happened. How could Nadia have written him? They were divided by fathoms of water, deprived of any and all radio communication. David often saw himself as a rescuer leaning from the prow of a salvage ship, a rescuer trying to make out the shape of a wrecked submarine on the ocean floor. If he didn't go back down as soon as possible, the world below was going to run out of oxygen—he was inexplicably sure of it. Nadia and Jorgo would start suffocating, their faces going blue; they'd collapse, clawing at their chests. Tormented by this fear, David kept watch for their SOS, but the mailbox remained empty, the telephone silent. Wasn't there any way through, a leak, a breach between the worlds? He alone could come and go while they remained prisoners, forever captives of a dimension with no exit. From time to time, when his loneliness reached its height, he'd fill his bathroom sink and stare at the still water with the insane hope of creating a passage, opening a channel. He kept telling himself that by concentrating he might manage to transform the stupid white porcelain scallop shell into a kind of magic mirror. He'd stare at the drain for an hour, expecting to see Nadia's little face lifted toward him, like a woman watching a plane pass by, high above, shielding her eyes from the sun with one hand.

"Need a breath of fresh air?" he'd shout. Could she tell it was him? What would he have looked like from below? Wouldn't there be something terrifying about a face suddenly bursting through the sky's blue skin to shout words the wind would warp? But the question of oxygen worried him for real. Soler Mahus had blamed it all on drugs, but David's suspicions went even further. He was convinced that in the diver's absence, the world below slowly withered away, went into necrosis like a limb that blood reached poorly, if at all. Every time he went down, he brought a little oxygen with him, and that oxygen revivified the people of the dream, restoring color to their skin. The drowned submarine was resupplied with air. The trapped crew members stopped gasping at last; Nadia's lips lost their awful bluish tinge, a beautiful red once more. Oh, if only he could know for sure! Meanwhile he stalked his apartment, hands behind his back, a captain pacing the bridge of a ship anchored at neap tide. There was no movement on the surface, and the pavement was too opaque to make out what was going on below, deep beneath its bituminous crust. Lean out the balcony all you wanted, but you wouldn't see a thing. His gaze ran smack into the asphalt as if into the water of a filthy pond. Nothing ever came floating up, not the slightest flotsam, the least slick of oil. No buoy. And all this time, the trapped crew of the lost submersible was slowly suffocating. David had a very hard time with these latent periods, but it wasn't in his power to dictate how often he dove. The phenomenon required a certain energy that built up unconsciously. So long as his tank wasn't full, there was no point in trying another foray into dream. He'd just be depleting his batteries without really sinking beneath the surface. Penetration could only take place when the nervous system was completely recharged. Only then would the blue depths of dream open, would he feel himself sucked toward the bottom, would he sink like a stone. And David knew the hour had not yet come to step over the ship's rail. His nerves weren't crackling, they seemed relaxed, limp, like the strings on an old tennis racket. When he touched things, he didn't feel that little crackle of static electricity at the ends of his nails that announced his internal battery was ready once more to short-circuit reality itself. He was flaccid, emptied out, condemned to wait, and that drove him crazy. Some divers resorted to drugs to speed up their process, but David didn't believe in those techniques, which smacked of charlatanry. Besides, chemical substances filtered directly into the world down below, its rivers and streams. Hadn't Soler Mahus said so? They ran from its faucets and stagnated at the bottoms of soda bottles, poisoning everything. No, he had to make do with waiting. And it was a long wait. Terribly long.

[7]

Days Gone By/
Somnambulist Thieves and
Nocturnal Visitors

Alone in the apartment, David brooded endlessly on his memories. They rose from the depths of his skull like a distant buzzing, a drift of bees converging on a target. They'd start out fuzzy, blurry, then sharpen and suddenly there they were, swarming him, refusing to go back into their box. It was, in large part, to flee his memories that David lingered at Antonine's, but the baker always wound up gently kicking him out for fear of harmful gossip at the shop. Then he would go home, a great floury loaf under each arm, like a sleepwalker careful to maintain his balance, and there he was, back with his memories. Oh, he tried to read, but snatches of the past would lie in ambush, waiting between the pages of old novels. Here was a ticket to a movie theater long since demolished, there a wrapper from a vanished brand of candy. These improvised bookmarks were like so many traps. They would each suddenly reveal themselves to be fraught with incredibly clear images of almost hallucinatory precision. He'd be leafing through No. 9 in the adventures of Special Agent XBY-00, and suddenly everything would come back to him: smells, colors . . . He saw Hugo again, his friend when he was twelve, the one they called Hugo Thundercalves at school because his calves were like a cyclist's. Hugo, a little centaur of the suburbs, joined at the hip to his bike, pant legs rolled up so as not to "catch a spot of grease." Yes, first came Hugo, his fat face gleaming with effort, and then the pampered, doctored bicycle he spent all this time fixing up and oiling. David had long harbored the conviction that Hugo slept with his bike, fists clenched around the handlebars, pedaling in the space under the covers. Hugo was training to become a pro. With astounding masochism for one so young, he crammed rocks in his schoolbag and launched himself at the steepest hills. People said he was the "son of a lush," a bit off his rocker. It was in large part thanks to Hugo that David could devote himself to the louche delights of theft. The idea had come to him just like that, without malice aforethought. One day he'd walked past the cluttered courtyard of Merlin, the bric-a-brac trader, and thought: "I have to steal something." A bedazzling, Pascalian revelation. From then on, his every thought was for the twisted, dented, unmatched objects that littered the tinker's lair. He started talking to Hugo about it, laying out the basis of what would become their Wednesday raids.

"You'll stay out front, on your two-wheeler, feet on the pedals," David whispered, "ready to go as soon as I come out running."

"Uh, feet?" Hugo objected. "I can't do both feet. I'll fall right over."

"I didn't mean literally." David was getting impatient. "I'll jump on in back and you take off downhill. No one'll be able to catch us."

Their eyes shone. In their imaginations, the bicycle suddenly took on the aspect of a curious mount, half-horse, half–scrap metal, carrying them in a cloud of dust toward the painted backdrop of the horizon. "Sure, hunky-dory," Hugo approved, "but in order to pedal like a champ I need to get my strength up. Can't you go buy me some nuclear suppositories?"

Suppositories that gave off nuclear energy were his other hobbyhorse. They came from obsessively reading an American comic during a bad throat infection that had kept him bedridden for more than a week. In the delirium of fever, Hugo had strangely lumped together superheroes, whose powers came straight from accidental exposure to radiation, and the antibiotic suppositories the family doctor had prescribed. Hugo was a nice kid, but a bit off his rocker, a fact of which David was occasionally reminded . . . especially when he had to walk into a pharmacy and ask for nuclear suppositories. He would've liked to sneak away, but Hugo would be standing right there at the window, trying to read his friend's lips. No chance now of lying to Hugo, or tricking him; David had no choice but to go through with it all—stammer his request while trying not to go poppy-red and look too much like a moron. Invariably, he would come out of the drugstore empty-handed.

"Well?" Hugo panted, quivering with impatience.

"Prescription only," David would lie. "They wouldn't give me any."

"Aw, darn!" the cyclist grumbled. "Don't worry, we'll try somewhere else. It's bound to work someday." And he would cross the name of the pharmacy off the endless list of dispensaries copied from the phone book.

Since the grown-ups were clearly against them, they had to resign themselves to undertaking their first raid without the help of nuclear suppositories, trusting themselves to Hugo's calves alone. David had come tearing into Merlin's courtyard just as the old man was nursing his second daily liter of wine, seized an old clock with a broken face, and turned on his heels to exit enemy territory before the junk dealer came out of his trance. No sooner was David over the doorsill than he leapt onto Hugo's bike rack as if onto a horse, fresh from robbing a bank . . . which is to say, horribly bruising his balls. The speed the bike picked up going down Commerce Street had seemed miraculous, and sent actual shivers of holy terror racing up their spines. Just before he went home, David had tossed the clock in a trash can. He didn't know what made him do it. A fit of extravagance? Maybe Hugo's craziness was catching? Would he go off his rocker too and start hitting up every pharmacy in town for nuclear suppositories?

The next week, they'd carried out another raid, and the week after that too, and . . . It was like a curse, a vicious cycle whose workings David didn't understand. He would pass by old Merlin's secondhand shop and *click*, something would go off, a sudden gluttony for that heap of shapeless old things all jumbled up together, those mountains of used tires, cast-iron skillets gray with ash, pipes that looked like mortar casings after a battle. Over all this hovered some undefinable smell, the smell of the past, of things so old they'd seen it all: the world and its secrets. David beelined for these marvels, hands outstretched like claws. He sneaked into enemy territory, dashing low to the cobblestones, hair on end with terror, his mind intent only on the loot and a quick U-turn. Hugo was no longer satisfied with covering their getaway; he grew more demanding, raising the bar a notch with each new incursion.

"Gotta go a bit farther each time," he decreed. "That pile of clocks is too easy. There's nothing but trash outside, the good stuff's hiding back there in the shed. No two ways about it, buddy, you've got to dive deeper." Dive deeper? David had risen to the challenge, filling his lungs with air like a pearl diver as he entered the secondhand shop. But Hugo was right: old Merlin kept his best finds all the way at the back of the hangar, the aged items he sold to antique dealers. But they always tossed the haul no matter what. As soon as they got their hands on it, it lost all value, stopped glittering—like gold gone suddenly to lead. They'd ditch it in a garbage can or by the side of the road. Hugo took a liking to the forays. They were just too much fun; old Merlin'd never corner them! Now David was stealing candlesticks, bronzes, statuettes of chipped marble. But these objects, carefully scoped out with his father's binoculars, so feverishly coveted, seemed ugly and soiled as soon as they were past the doors of the junk shop. It was as if some magic charm governed fat old Merlin's territory.

"Don't you get it?" David muttered one day. "That's why he doesn't even bother to stop us. He knows everything we steal becomes worthless the minute it falls into our hands. He's a wizard."

"You're getting as crazy as I am," Hugo snickered. Then he added, "True, it looks a lot nicer inside. Maybe you're not going deep enough, is all."

Two weeks after that conversation, David became aware that his mother was also a shoplifter. The discovery astounded him. They didn't want for anything back home; David's father, a salesman, worked for a company that specialized in installing wall safes. His clientele consisted almost entirely of small business owners he called on from one end of the country to the other, hardly ever setting foot back at home more than twice a month. Mama was tall and thin, but pretty, with a face like a ferret lost in a thicket of blonde hair she never managed to tame. She didn't talk much, and spent whole afternoons deep in an armchair, wearing nothing but a lace slip, smoking cigarette after cigarette. The room became blue around her, filling with a suffocating fog. When she spoke, bitter scrolls of smoke escaped her lips, as if from the jaws of a dragon slumbering in a fairy tale. Bored, she would cast about for a quarter of an hour, chewing on her nails with their flaking polish, then dive back into the movie magazines that were all she read. Whenever David tried to speak to her, she would muss his hair and murmur gently, "Poor darling boy, I've got a migraine. You picked a bad day. Let's talk about it some other time."

She was never mean, or sullen, never yelled or scolded. But each time he tried to make contact, she withdrew with a sad, impish grin as if just being near other people chafed her skin. "Poor darling boy . . ." she'd begin, and drift off.

She always had a migraine. Later, she went so far as to use the word "period," because it was surer to send a terrified David running. Her hands, clothes, and hair smelled of smoke. She drifted barefoot from one room to the next in a pink silk slip, her pack of cigarettes and lighter in hand. It was a big soldier's lighter, nickel-plated, on which had been engraved a somewhat terrifying inscription David never tired of trying to fathom.

Madame Zara. Clairvoyant. Psychic readings, summoning of the deceased, speaking with the dead. He'd questioned Mama more than once about the origins of this phrase without ever getting an answer. "She's just a lady," she said one day, evasively. "A lady I used to work for before I met your father." That was all he ever found out.

Mama stole from department stores. She probably always had, but David—too young then, and too distracted by the spectacle of toys—had never noticed before. Mama stole nonchalantly, as if in a trance, without even trying to look around and make sure there were no guards. She stole as if sleepwalking, vanishing objects up her sleeves like a music hall prestidigitator. David was convinced she got rid of the fruit of her larceny just like he did. This discovery persuaded him they both suffered from the same hereditary disease . . . perhaps even a curse. He spoke to no one about it, not even Hugo. Watching his mother, he realized she had no fear of being caught red-handed. She probably had some magic charm that made her legerdemain invisible to the eyes of salesclerks and plainclothes cops. He took great pride in this, and considered himself a fool for having trembled even a moment for her sake. She was good, real good. She could've whisked an entire store into her pockets without anyone being any the wiser. *She had a gift.* Besides, she moved as if possessed; you could tell from the glassy look in her eyes when she tucked an item up her sleeve.

Whenever Mama operated, salesclerks and customers became blind. Morillard, head of the plainclothes division, took to wheeling around the various departments like a bat deranged by the light. He was a sight to see, eyes wild, the few hairs he had left pasted down with brilliantine, and his little mustache perched precariously above his spindly upper lip, circling like a hound flustered by the wind, a hound that had lost the scent of its prey. His instincts told him something was going on *right under his nose,* but he didn't know where. David would hear the detective whistling behind his back; he could even smell the vegetable soup under the man's cheap aftershave. Morillard kept circling, circling, a myopic matador looking vainly about for the bull . . . and Mama would fill her pockets with rings, bracelets that she never wound up wearing. David was proud of her. When he thought about it, he always wound up wondering if he and Mama weren't one of those doomed couples in noir novels. He was drunk with impunity. There was nothing he enjoyed watching so much as her sauntering unhurried from a department store, pockets full of glittering costume junk torn from the display case. The cherry on top, the thumb to the nose, was when she'd stop right in front of the cops ready to ambush her at the exit and take her sweet time

knotting a scarf around her neck like an honest citizen beyond reproach. He had the feeling shoplifting was just the beginning, that
soon he and Mama would really go wild and take this town to the
cleaners. They'd become kingpins. There'd be no crime too low:
blackmail, murder . . . No one would know what they looked like.
By day they'd stroll down the avenues, hand in amiable hand, but
by night—ah, by night! Faces hidden under scarlet cowls, they'd
sow terror, eviscerating the safes of the leisured class, and the leisured classes themselves if those old buggers made so much as a
move to call for help.

They'd scour the town, making it cough up all its ill-gotten
gains, and no one would be any the wiser. It'd be their secret. In
the meantime, they shoplifted: Mama in department stores, David at the junk shop. They were in fact very close to each other,
even if they never talked about it. Their connivance simply lay on
another level, deeper, more mysterious, where words were no use.
Sometimes David wondered where Mama had learned to steal so
skillfully. Had she been part of a ring of pilfering youths trained
in secret schools by masters lighter-fingered than magicians? He'd
read a novel about it and, for a few days, had felt an actual voca-
tional call for pickpocketing. In reality, he knew nothing about
Mama's past. She never brought it up, never said, "When I was
your age . . ." What ties bound her to the strange Madame Zara
whose name was engraved on her lighter, a lady who specialized
in summoning the dead?

During one raid on the junk shop, things took a sudden turn.
Just as David leapt onto Hugo's bike rack, old man Merlin burst
from his shack and hurled a jankety alarm clock at David's head.

The chunk of metal struck the boy in the temple, throwing him from the seat. Half-unconscious, David rolled across the cobblestones while his buddy took off, shrieking with terror, nose pressed to the handlebars to duck the wind on the way down Commerce Street. The junkman seized David by the scruff of his neck like a cat he was about to drown, demanded his address, and, without another word, dragged him home. Bad timing: Dad had just come back from his rounds and was getting ready to enjoy a long weekend with his feet up in slippers. The confrontation was a horrible one. The scrap collector laid out in great detail every single incursion the "little rapscallion" had made. He'd established a daunting (and highly exaggerated) list of objects plundered. He demanded compensation on the spot, or he'd go and press charges. Dad paid; his face was livid as candle wax. When old Merlin was gone, he advanced on David, slowly unbuckling his belt with the clear intent of using it as a whip, but Mama intervened.

"Touch a hair on his head, and I'm out of here," she said in a flat voice. "I won't say it again. You know it's not his fault. It's because of his gift. I've explained this all to you before."

Dad seemed to lose his head then, and began shouting things that made no sense. He called Mama a witch, a psycho, and said she'd be better off going back to work at her circus of lunatics. Mama made no reply. She sat back down in the old armchair and lit her cigarette, shrouding herself in blue smoke as if to weave a fuliginous veil between herself and the rest of the world. Dad kept shouting by his lonesome for a good part of the night, then buckled his suitcases and left, shouting over his shoulder that he was happier at a hotel anyway, rather than in this stinking dump . . .

and if it kept up, he'd never set foot back here again. David's throat was so tight with fear he couldn't even cry. When Dad's car drove off, Mama pulled him onto her lap and mussed his hair.

"It's not your fault," she said in that voice tarry with tobacco, which grew raspier with each passing year. "It's a side effect of the gift. When God gives you a present, a power, a talent, the Devil also hands you a poisoned apple, so as not to be outdone. You have to deal with them both. Pay for your gift with a vice, a defect—that's the rule. Some people become perverts, others murderers. No point complaining; our cross isn't all that hard to bear. Stealing isn't the worst thing. I know others who've had to give into much more disgusting weaknesses."

David didn't understand much of what she was saying. What gift? He wasn't bad at drawing (especially naked women), but it wasn't enough to make a big deal about. He couldn't sing, much less dance. He was in no way artistically inclined. So what, then?

As if the failure of the last raid had upset the very order of the world, Mama got nabbed by fat old Morillard right during the annual clearance sales. David let out a whimper of fear when the cop's hand pounced on his mother's wrist in the costume jewelry department, and for a second, he thought he'd wet his pants like a baby.

"Little lady," chuckled the brilliantined, mustachioed man, "I think we have a lot to discuss. We go way back, don't we? You've been playing me for a sap for quite a while. Now you're coming with me to my office for a quick pat-down."

David followed as if in a dream. No one had spoken a word to him, and he'd never felt so small. He knew if he opened his mouth, he'd immediately burst out sobbing. Morillard ushered them down a dark, narrow hall.

"Kid, you sit your butt down and don't move!" he ordered, indicating a flaking cast-iron chair. Then he pushed Mama into the office and closed the door neatly behind him.

"Now, about that pat-down," he crowed, delighted. "First, empty your pockets. Then your sleeves!"

The ringing in David's ears blotted out what followed, but at one point the cop yelled: "I said your slip too!" Then there was a muddled noise, as if things were falling on the floor. Mama came out ten minutes later. Her face was smeared with lipstick and her hair disheveled. She took David by the hand and left the store standing tall, in no hurry, as if indifferent to the salesladies' looks.

"So, um," David stammered once they were outside. The winter evening shrouded the street in darkness. "We're not going to jail?"

"No," Mama murmured, "you can always cut a deal with a guy like that. You have to take your punishment without flinching. It's because of the gift. They make us atone for it on credit. That's how it is. It'll be the same way with you. Every now and then, they'll hand you a bill, and you'll have to pay up, no balking."

When they were back at the house, Mama hurried to the shower and stayed under the water for a long time. When at last she emerged from the bathroom, wrapped in her old dressing gown, she downed three sleeping pills with a glass of rum and went to bed. David alone remained awake in the empty house, unable to sleep. Something had been broken, but he didn't know what. Was it his fault Mama had gotten caught? Had the failure of his last raid derailed the delicate gears that had till now ensured them utter impunity? It was his fault; he'd let his guard down. Success had gone to his head. He'd underestimated old Merlin, and . . .

That same night, he heard his mother let out a moan. Thinking she was sick, he peeked through the door to his parents' room. It was something he'd never done before, but the image of the sleeping pills suddenly came back to mind. What if Mama had poisoned herself? What if—

She lay on her back, eyes closed. From her open mouth rose a white, almost luminous plume of smoke that coiled in the air and formed a pudgy sphere like a ball of yarn up by the ceiling. At first he thought it was cigarette smoke, but it didn't smell like tobacco. The air smelled strange, *electric*. He took a step toward the bed, his hands icy. Mama was fast asleep, and smoke kept leaking from her open mouth as if she were burning up inside. Timidly, David poked it with his index finger. The smoke had a weird, gummy consistency. Not only was it warm, but it was also stretchy, *palpable*. The ball by the ceiling was now big around as a balloon, and bumps were forming on its surface. It was like . . . a kind of sculpture. A ball of white dough, sculpting itself. It was . . . a head. A human head . . .

The head of fat old Morillard. David ran out of the room, too terrified to even scream. The white head followed him, caught in the updraft of his flight. David didn't know where to hide. Morillard's head was hovering in the hallway, bobbing like a balloon on the whim of the breeze. The pale, moonlike face didn't seem to be alive. Rather, it looked like a flying sculpture that an ever more tenuous string tied to Mama's mouth.

"She barfed that thing!" David thought as he curled up under the coffee table. "It's just flying puke, is all!"

He tried to reason with himself to contain his fear as the gruesome head fluttered this way and that, crashing into doors, bouncing back. This went on for a few minutes, then it burst with a curious pop, like a soap bubble, spraying David with a bizarre substance that reminded him of marshmallow.

This time he needed an answer. The next day, he went to Mama and told her what had happened that night. The young woman seemed surprised by his ignorance. "But, sweetie," she burst out laughing, "that's *the gift*. I thought you knew. Hasn't it ever happened to you before? We're mediums! We materialize ectoplasms."

"Ecto-whats?"

"Ectoplasms. Back in the day, people believed they were images of the dead. But they're just models drawn from our dreams. Mental images that solidify in the air while we sleep. It's as if dreams came out of people through their ears and turned into creatures of smoke."

David frowned, digesting this information. "So that was your job with Madame Zara?" he asked. "You summoned dead people?"

"Oh, that's just what Auntie Zara told people," Mama giggled. "Before each séance, she'd give me a photo of the deceased, whomever the customer wanted to see. I'd concentrate on it, to memorize the facial features, then Zara would hypnotize me and put me to sleep, commanding me to dream about what I'd just seen. Then the face would come out of my mouth and start floating around the room. The customers were really happy, convinced they were actually dealing with ghosts. It was kind of a con job, sweetie. I couldn't really summon the dead, I just sculpted their heads out of smoke. That's how I met your father. He came every week so I could bring back one of his old mistresses who died in a car accident. For a long time, he really believed I was a witch. When I tried to set him straight, he was very disappointed."

David was puzzled. So that was the gift? Was he also going to start vomiting up faces that exploded like soap bubbles? That was stupid! Moronic! Pointless! Only good for a circus sideshow. And for this ability, so utterly devoid of interest, they were doomed to theft?

"I was never very talented," Mama went on to herself. "My ectoplasms never lasted very long. They burst too quickly, and sometimes they also lost their shape, became hideous. That caused a lot of trouble with the customers. I couldn't maintain the consistency of the features long enough. The noses get huge, the ears like an elephant's. Zara would bawl me out when I came to. She'd scream, 'God Almighty, just think about what you're doing!' But it would all start all over again with the next séance."

Actually, Mama wasn't really sure what the gift was good for. Until now, mediums had been used in the occult sector. A skilled shaper of ectoplasms working at a respectable practice could make a good living. Outside of that narrow professional niche, the job market was zilch.

"But I don't want to work for a witch!" protested David. "Not even for pretend. Puking up dead people is gross!"

Mama shrugged. All she knew was David would have the gift,

just as she herself had gotten it from her mother, and he'd just have to live with it. He alone could decide if it was worth trying to cash in on. David felt oddly swindled. In the space of a second he'd gone from being a wizard to a carnival mountebank—hardly a pleasant sensation. In the weeks that followed, this curious legacy came up a few more times in conversation, then Mama fell back into her usual silence. Papa hardly ever came home anymore; rumor had it he was on the other side of the country with "another family" where he felt more at home. This parallel household plunged David into confusion. He tried to imagine his father with another woman, another child. At first, in a fit of anger, he'd thought: "But we're his real family." Now he was no longer sure. It seemed to him that Papa's absence, his brief and ever more infrequent visits, attenuated the reality of their bonds, turning him and Mama into understudies confined to the wings. The real family was "the other one," those strangers who lived at the antipodes. David and Mama were but shadows . . . ectoplasms with transparent flesh.

When he turned fourteen, David began vomiting up his first ghosts. It happened at night, without his knowing. In the morning he'd find the hodgepodges floating by the ceiling like balloons at a party. Unlike his mother, he gave birth to nonrepresentational but persistent amalgams that were a long time breaking up.

"Poor darling boy," Mama murmured, "those don't look like anything. They're like . . . popcorn. And here I was going to introduce you to Madame Zara."

His mother's disappointment made David unhappy, but at the same time he was relieved he wouldn't have to work for some occultist charlatan.

"A medium who can't shape a likeness," Mama despaired. "If that doesn't beat all."

With touching stubbornness, she tried to correct her son, giving him advice like a coach. She showed him photos, forcing him to memorize them, but David never produced anything resembling a "likeness," just unidentifiable abstract forms.

"You puke Picassos," Mama sighed. "If you can find a customer with that kind of face, you'll be in luck." But David didn't want to get mixed up in scamming the living. The idea of becoming a great thief was as attractive to him as the idea of being a con man was repulsive. Between the ages of seventeen and twenty he produced a great many ectoplasms, especially when he was in love or under sexual stress. Papa came back to live with them when he learned that Mama wasn't doing so well. The doctors had found something in her lung, some nasty disease from smoking too much, but David knew they were wrong. It was an ectoplasm that had balled itself up inside Mama's chest. When you started getting old, the damn gunk got thicker and thicker till it wouldn't come out. It stuck to your bronchial tubes and hardened. Mama was dying because a stillborn ghost was clogging up her lungs. When Papa came back, he'd grown old, as if his "real" family, the one at the antipodes, had worn him out unreasonably.

Between the ages of twenty and twenty-three, David went through a latency period and thought he'd lost his gift. He was relieved. For three years, he'd systematically avoided spending the night with a girl for fear a ghost would come out of his mouth while he was asleep, which didn't exactly help his love life. Women complained that he ran off as soon as he'd shot his wad, and called him a prick. But what else could he do? For three years, he led a normal life. Then the phenomenon started up again, less frequent now but more elaborate. From then on, he produced strangely beautiful structures which, when he happened to leave a few lying around in a corner of the apartment, seemed to cast a spell over visitors and hold them in curious thrall.

Once Mama was buried, Papa left again to find his real family, leaving behind no address, no telephone number, as if the antipodes enjoyed no modern means of communication. David let him go without lifting a finger.

That was the year people started talking about the first therapeutic sculptures. The papers were full of articles boasting the merit of these healing statues. The fashion for these curious abstract assemblages, executed in a material hitherto unknown to visual artists, was all the rage in America. One glance at a magazine photo and David knew they were ectoplasms. Curiously tortured ectoplasms, like the ones he'd been producing since he was a teenager.

[8]

Bad News in Bliss Plaza

David crossed the museum esplanade, listening to the echo of his steps under the archways. The sound always made him feel like he was being pursued by a legion of invisible men hiding behind the tall pillars. No matter how fast he turned around, he never managed to surprise these ghosts as they moved about (but how could he have, if they were invisible?). The feeling of being surrounded finally became oppressive, like a trap he couldn't locate but knew was closing in all around. That morning, he'd felt an urge to go see Soler Mahus's magnum opus again, the one on display in Bliss Plaza, in the open air. On the way back, he'd stop by and see Marianne in her tiny office in the medical section.

He went down the long marble steps. The great dream took up the entire surface of the former reflecting pool, unfurling its shapes and curves like a strange aerodynamic transport waiting to take flight. A living machine, a celestial seashell, or even . . . a cloud, maybe, a cloud beached on the ground after long drifting on the jet streams. A captive cloud? Marooned like a whale come to die on the beach, its sonar on the blink.

The sculpture burgeoned, taking up a good hundred square yards. Contemplating it, you wondered how one man alone could have given birth to an ectoplasm of such size without it costing him his life. But that was no doubt why Soler was old beyond his years, why little by little he'd come to look like a living mummy unable to so much as wiggle his pinky. His outsize dreams had sucked the marrow from his bones, withering his body, tanning his flesh into leather stiffer than jerky. His life essence was gone, consumed by dream. David knew that ectoplasms wore your body out. Each time he managed to bring something back from the depths of dream, he lost weight, as if the object expelled through his mouth corresponded to an actual portion of flesh. Each time he stepped on the scale after a dive, he was convinced he'd undergone a mysterious amputation. Something had been taken away from him, he didn't know what; it was painless, and yet his anatomy was no longer complete. Each dream consumed an organ. Sometimes this idea took on obsessive proportions. For the ectoplasms were not made of smoke, as he'd initially believed; further veterinary studies had shown their texture to be composed of living cells suspended in a very loosely structured protoplasmic compound. Some popular science magazines had even compared ectoplasms to benign growths that developed literally outside the subject. This rather unappealing view of the process, which reduced dreams to the approximate level of mere warts, had not, however, cooled the public's enthusiasm. David often thought of the emaciated Soler Mahus, looking like a recently unwrapped Egyptian mummy. The ectoplasms had eaten him alive. His children had carved themselves bodies from his very flesh, leaving him but bones, skin, and just enough organs to lead the life of a vegetable, reduced to a few basic functions. It was his flesh spread out there for all to see, on Bliss Plaza. His organs—sublimated, purified, rid of their ugly visceral materiality, but his organs all the same . . . David had no illusions. These days, an art gallery was nothing but a monstrous anatomical display. Below each work the following inscription might as well have been engraved: *shaped from the artist's liver.* But the public would probably not have appreciated this overly organic truth.

He stopped at the foot of the steps. The prodigious size of the ectoplasm terrified him. He had but to close his eyes a brief second to see Soler, melting like a candle, consuming himself in a sizzle of hot wax to give birth to this monstrosity—so beautiful, and so poignant.

The great dream was, in fact, a state commission. When people spoke of it, they called it "the sculpture that stopped the war," for that was indeed what had happened. Time and again, journalists had told the story of how Soler had been flown in a helicopter to the front line between two warring nations on the verge of a bloodbath. In a single night, he'd shaped this dream whose benign radiance had put an end to the homicidal impulses of both sides, and order was restored. A truce was declared, treaties were signed, and finally peace had returned and everyone gave themselves a shake as if coming out of a nightmare, wondering with worry-tinged disbelief why it had almost come to mass murder.

The great dream that had stopped the war had sat enthroned on Bliss Plaza for five years. Though it showed a few tiny signs of fading, it was far from withering away. Its presence had driven up the apartment prices in the neighborhood, everyone wanting to live close to the work to benefit from its soothing emanations. Health services had conducted statistical studies that proved residents in buildings overlooking Bliss Plaza were wholly free of psychosomatic complaints, and enjoyed excellent health. Better still: incurable diseases had completely vanished in a three-hundred-yard radius around the oneiric object. The lucky few lived with their windows open, naked most of the time to offer up as much of their bodies as possible to the miraculous rays it gave off. A stroll in the nearby streets was all it took to tell the people here were much more beautiful than anywhere else. Their flesh was sound, their features lissome and easeful. Not a single line showed on their skin, and a trace of gray hair was the exception that proved the rule. Visitors were dumbstruck by the sight of children playing naked in midwinter in the snow along the avenue's balconies, but no one around here feared colds, throat infections, pleurisy anymore. Their bodies no longer knew the tyrannies of such afflictions from a darker age. There was always something slightly dreamlike about the sight of these nudists of all sexes wandering past open windows in luxurious interiors appointed by the best decorators, but not a single one of them would've run the risk of concealing some part of his body, having it miss out on the rays from the sculpture and, as a result, age faster than the rest. Those without the means to rent apartments nearby made pilgrimages to Bliss Plaza whenever their schedules allowed. Sundays the museum esplanade was carpeted by a silent, naked crowd sprawled on the steps and grass. They exposed themselves to the benefits of the sculpture just as they had once persisted in sunning themselves on beaches colonized by paid vacation time. David found the silent, smiling crowd slightly alarming. Like all professional dreamers, he was impervious to the power of oneiric objects. Draped in his wrinkled old raincoat, he tried to beat a path through all the breasts, all the members generously offered up. Weren't these people cold?

"At least now we know what art is for," an old woman had told him. "Back in the day, we used to say, 'It's beautiful.' But what does that even mean? Beauty never stopped me from getting hemorrhoids. Now it's different, there's nothing to understand. It's like vitamins. I have no idea what it's supposed to be, but it does me good!"

David made his way slowly around the dream. Though he admired it as a feat of prowess, he felt in no way flooded by euphoria or good health. This aspect of things remained unavailable to him. He was like a deaf worker who made hi-fi stereos. He knew all the mechanics, but couldn't enjoy them because of a mysterious infirmity that no doctor was able to explain.

As he readied to head toward the museum, he suddenly spotted Marianne coming toward him, a case file under her arm. She was wearing her usual gray outfit: shapeless skirt and sweater, worn-out flats. Her bun made the bones of her skinny face stick out.

"I saw you from the window in my office," she said. "This is a better place for a chat."

David frowned. What was she hoping for? That the sculpture would elate them both, easing the passage of an especially bitter pill? Or maybe she was the one who needed some fleeting anesthesia from her stress to deliver what David could already tell was bad news?

"Your last dream was designated a no-pass," she blurted, mumbling slightly. "It didn't survive the anti-allergy injections. The biohazard tests weren't encouraging either. Apparently you had a close brush with nightmare during that last dream? You were scared, and the dream object was suffused with adrenaline, something the lab is afraid will have a negative effect on potential buyers."

David grimaced. A no-pass meant it would never leave quarantine.

"You know the mandatory precautions," Marianne murmured. "Too much adrenaline amounts to saying your work is poison. Unfit for consumption. Safety standards are very strict. We don't want customers traumatized by high-stress radiation breathing down our necks. You're tired, David. All this dreaming is wearing you out. You have to stop and take some time off for a while."

The young man stood before her, staring right into her eyes. She didn't blink. The nearness of the sculpture cleansed her of her habitual tics. Her lips weren't pursed, like usual. Her whole face seemed relaxed, at voluptuous ease. She was even almost . . . beautiful? She spoke in a slack voice, making no attempt for once to browbeat her listener. *It's her, and at the same time, someone else*, he thought, *a kind of twin sister who just slipped out . . .*

"I'm sorry, David," she said, "but we're taking you out of the running for a while. Your last few dreams have all died in the incubators. Plus, the objects you're producing are just getting smaller and smaller; what they bring in barely covers the warehousing costs. We can't put them up at auction anymore, and gift shops rarely carry them. If you can't get ahold of yourself soon, it's big-box stores for you from here on out; your dreams will be sold in the aisle with the air fresheners. You don't want that to happen, do you?"

David shrugged. "Quarantine's a slaughterhouse," he grumbled. "Any dream that's at all delicate doesn't make it. Your batteries of tests would stop a tank dead in its tracks."

"You know that's not true!" the young woman said with aggravating patience. "Besides, that's not all there is to it. Most dreams are sold with a one-year warranty. Yours wither so fast we had to cut it back to six months. Now we'll have to reduce our coverage to ninety days. People just don't trust objects with really short warranties, you know that. They feel like they've just sunk their money into rubbish. You aren't selling, David. You have to get back in shape. Give up diving for a year; it'll do you a world of good."

"You can't just turn it on and off. You go where it leads you."

"Don't be such a romantic! Even if we don't fully understand the ectoplasmic creative process, we can at least suppress it. All it takes is an injection, a quick shot, and you won't be able to dream for twelve months. Of course, we can't force it on you. But from now on, you won't have psychological monitoring during trance periods. No one will come watch over you while you're dreaming. You know what that means?"

David nodded. To dive unassisted was to run the risk of sinking into a weeklong trance, sometimes more, with no medical supervision. That meant no glucose drip, pure fasting, dehydration. Many divers had died that way, starving or dehydrated, while deep in a dream.

"The Ministry's policy gives priority to big dreams," Marianne murmured, turning to Soler Mahus's ectoplasmic sculpture. "I know the government would like to install similar monuments at every intersection. We're looking for the next Soler. You make trinkets, David. Fashion isn't on your side. Trinkets belong to an age when the public conceived of dreams only as an intimate and solitary experience. These days, people gather together to enjoy works collectively. They commune in a shared passion for serenity."

"No, keep going," David snickered. "Don't hold back. Say what you were thinking. I know the military's interested in dreams. Ever since Soler Mahus stopped that war, the top brass has been busy trying to figure a way to weaponize dreams. I know some of them even wanted to materialize nightmares capable of scaring potential enemies to death."

"Those are just rumors," Marianne cut him off with a frightened blink. "I'd advise you not to share them with anyone."

"Another rumor is that the nightmare objects were so terrifying they resulted in the deaths of the divers and the officers overseeing the experiment. True?"

Marianne put her hand on David's arm. "I know you think I'm a pain in the neck," she said with a sad smile, "but I'm very fond of you. Don't try to dive alone. You know what'll happen: you'll fall into a coma and your vital functions will fail one after another. Let me give you the shot that will keep you from going under."

But the young man was no longer listening. Fists shoved deep in his pockets, he gazed at the great sculpture through half-lidded eyes. "So that's what you go for, huh?" he jeered. "Art that soothes and pacifies. Above all, nothing tortured, nothing that comes out of a crisis, nothing fed by despair. That's what quarantine is for: triage. You poison everything that might potentially disturb the public."

"Don't get paranoid! Some dream objects are harmful to your health. There have been cases of contamination. People who went into depression after being exposed to rays from an unauthorized novelty."

"If you won't have me, I'll go work for the parallel circuit."

"The black market? You'd be working in a complete breach of the law. Dreams marketed without veterinary sanction? That's like what controlled substances used to be. Don't get caught up in that trap; you'll wind up in prison. It's not our fault if your dreams keep withering away ever faster. You know the rest cure won't cost you a dime; it's in your contract. You have a right to a six-month stay at a therapeutic establishment every five years."

"You call that a vacation?" David hissed. "They probably think of good old manual labor as physical therapy! Give everyone a pickax and a section of road to build!"

Marianne remained impassive, even smiling faintly. The nearness of the giant ectoplasm kept her from losing her temper. Her mood stayed even no matter what came out of his mouth. *Fuck!* he suddenly felt like shouting. *You filthy slut! You dumb cunt! You frigid bitch!* He knew she'd greet these abominations with the same indulgent little smile. She looked like a patient in pre-anesthesia. He could've hacked off one of her limbs, and she wouldn't have made a sound. He turned and left before doing something he couldn't take back.

In a café, he had three glasses of milk, then went over to see Soler Mahus, but the old dreamer didn't recognize him, and didn't open his mouth. They'd shaved his head, and his bare skin betrayed unsettling bumps that distended his cranium. It was as if something was trapped under the glacier of his skull, trying desperately to tear through the seams and make its way outside. David stayed at the artist's bedside for half an hour, till a nurse shooed him off.

Miserable and exhausted, he dragged himself to Antonine's. With an embarrassed look, the baker confessed she'd just chucked one of his dreams in the trash.

"It withered last night," she whispered. "It was even starting to smell."

[9]

Underground Snow for
a Secret Burial

Maybe he should've married Antonine, gotten back into normal life, given up the art that had made him live on the margins of the world for too long? He often tried to imagine what his life would have been like with the plump baker. It didn't take much to see himself in a cardigan, face dusted with flour, kneading dough in the darkest hours of the night. He'd shape the stretchy dough, turning it into even boules, cocoons of crumb asking only to be hardened by the hot breath of the wood-fired oven. Yes, a normal life, one that left you with an aching lumbar and seized-up shoulders, but so very fulfilled. At dawn, with the batch done, he'd have stepped into the courtyard out back for a cigarette and watched the sunrise, watched the windows in the nearby buildings light up one by one. Antonine . . . or Marianne? Why not Marianne?

Didn't she become strangely sociable as soon as she stepped into the aura of a dream? All he'd have to do was fill the apartment with dream knickknacks. At night, when she came home from work, the dreams heaped on the shelves would wipe the bad mood right off her face. In a few seconds, she'd be carefree as a little girl again, ready to laugh at anything, to have fun at the drop of a hat. Thus anesthetized, she'd become someone else; even her angular figure, all skin and bone, would seem to soften, round out. Yes, maybe he should've turned in his art worker's license, and just dreamed for himself alone, with no end in mind other than lightening Marianne's chronic bad moods? Maybe . . . or else quit this filthy habit for good, let his powers atrophy by deliberately refraining from practice, like a bodybuilder watching his splendid musculature melt away as soon as he stops working the barbells? Amputate that unhealthy part of himself; wait for his brain to rust and stiffen till it produced nothing but run-of-the-mill dreams, dreams like the ones that haunted the sleep of Mr. Average Joe? Oh, to dream at last of dumb, inconsequential little things, woolly nonsense that didn't force its way out of his body to become works of art. To dream of things that would fade away all by themselves when he woke and not stubbornly linger in reality, like ineradicable clues in an absurd crime. Well, then? Antonine? Marianne? A woman of flesh and a woman of bones . . . either was better than Nadia, that ghost he could never embrace, right?

That morning, the doorbell yanked him from his thoughts as he mulled, as was his habit, elbows on the table, face bent over a mug of coffee, spying on his reflection in the black liquid. An ill-shaven telegram boy, his hat on sideways, handed him a cable from the veterinary services of the Museum of Modern Art. The rectangle of blue paper informed him that due to medical testing prior to being approved for the market, the dream he had submitted to quarantine a few days ago had just passed away. As per his contract, he had the right to attend burial proceedings for the object.

He wasn't really surprised. Marianne had prepared him for this outcome, but still, he couldn't keep from crumpling the telegram with rage. No-pass. From now on he'd be classified as a no-passer, a dreamer whose oneiric objects couldn't stand up to quarantine. The crude, stupid stamp would sprawl in runny letters all over his file. To take his mind off things, he shaved methodically with the straight razor his father had left in the medicine cabinet fifteen years ago. A delicate operation, it required all his attention, and even kept him from brooding on dark thoughts. His face wrapped in a hot towel, he waited for the burning in his cheeks to die down, then put on his black suit. The suit he found himself wearing ever more often. He remained seated in his armchair for a long time, flipping with a nervous finger through a little novel whose binding was coming off. It recounted the adventures of Dr. Skeleton in Patagonia. He knew it almost by heart, but was always amused by the part, beloved by fans, when the formidable doctor formed an army of kamikaze soldiers by hypnotizing gorillas from the nearby jungle. He wound up falling asleep in his mourning wear, tie knotted, legs spread, like a dead man who'd broken out of his coffin. He only came out of it fifteen minutes before the ceremony, and had to hurry to the museum. The fat old

watchman he so often bribed met him at the service entrance of
the veterinary clinic with a fitting scowl. David heard not a word
of the usual expressions of commiseration and crossed the storage
chamber toward the incubators. The sanitation men were already
there, in their black rubber suits, gloved and booted like sewage
workers. David knew all too well that many of them were former dreamers dismissed because they'd stopped turning a profit.
In order to spare them the vagrancy that usually followed such a
discharge, the Administration, like a child seeing dutifully to an
aging parent, had suggested they retrain for what was discreetly
known as the *removal service for withered oneiric objects*. A name
that seemed to turn them into florists charged with gathering up
faded bouquets at the end of official ceremonies. Though he understood their distress and the awkwardness of their situation, David
could not help but think of these men as traitors, vandals abusing
their status to despoil works of art with impunity. He had sworn
never to submit to such reeducation. Even now, the garbagemen of
dreams, stuffed into their rubbery outfits, looked like giant frogs
trained to stand on their hind legs. A hood perforated with giant
glass eyeholes completed the outfit and put a finishing touch on the
resemblance. David nodded to them. One of them, Pit Van Larsen,
with whom he'd used to hang out, nodded back. They put out their
cigarettes, pulled the flabby masks down over their faces, and approached the incubators. The dead dreams sagged beneath the bell
jars like limp salads. They were still just as immaculately white,
but they had altered in density. Their fine texture had coarsened,
and had transmogrified into a gooey substance that was extremely
difficult to manipulate. Personnel were highly discouraged from

seizing a dream bare-handed if they didn't want to find themselves glued to whatever it had been sitting on. Oneiric objects had frightening adhesive powers. When they were first put on the market, the Ministry had to deal with many accidents, and rescue teams crisscrossed the cities in every direction, twenty-four hours a day, to bail out unfortunate souls who'd found themselves fastened to their mantel or buffet while trying to sweep a withered dream away with the back of a hand. Disintegrating ectoplasmic matter adored human skin and hardened instantaneously upon contact, turning into a fearsome cement. In such cases, careless victims were rarely freed without recourse to a razor and local anesthetic. The instructions that came with all oneiric objects specified that disposing of sculptures at the first sign of rot was highly advised. The recommended method was simple: all it involved was being sure to slip on a pair of rubber gloves (household gloves for washing dishes would do nicely) before seizing the shriveled ectoplasm and placing it in a tear-proof plastic bag. In each building a special receptacle had been installed for express use with dreams. It was a big black rubber cylinder whose lid opened and closed automatically at the press of a red button. The very peculiar nature of persistent ectoplasms had necessitated this amenity, and it would have been naïve to consider it a pointlessly precautionary luxury. Indeed, dreams in full-blown decline were almost unmanageable. Though they lost their shape and their suggestive power—in short, their beauty—their substance survived, incompressible. It did not shrink or evaporate. Grown flaccid and sticky, dreams stood up to the most powerful means of disposal. At first, attempts were made to burn them like dead leaves, but incinerating them gave rise to a pestilential, intensely toxic smoke whose effluvia had resulted in several cases of poisoning, and even a few deaths.

To top it all off, smoldering dreams reeked of burnt flesh. At their slightest touch, the smallest backyard brazier became a stake from the Holy Inquisition, and the smell of charred human flesh the ectoplasms let off impregnated clothes almost permanently, necessitating a change of wardrobe. That disposal method had to be scrapped, and people to be persuaded not to try to deal with withered objects on their own. And so a removal service was created, a service whose black trucks patrolled town at nightfall to collect the ectoplasms standing in bins on the sidewalks among the innocent family trash cans.

"Let's do this," was all Pit Van Larsen said, pulling his mask over his face. David took a cautious step back. Splashing was always a possibility; he didn't particularly feel like having a pearl of gummy matter leap his way and stick to his skin like a wart, as sometimes happened.

Since collecting dreams posed a real problem, allowing them to decompose in the open air of landfills like regular household trash was out of the question, for as the weeks went by and they fell apart, ectoplasms wound up unraveling in sticky, invisible tendrils in the wind. Scattered, reduced to a state like microscopic droplets of rain, they then became windborne. Those unlucky enough to live near landfills breathed them in, absorbed them unknowingly. And the terrifyingly sticky particles built up in their lungs and bronchial tubes, permanently obstructing them. Eventually, the Ministry had had to face facts: dead dreams were exceptional sources of pollution. They'd rather glibly thought the problem solved for a while when the strange raw material was recycled in a less-than-noble, but highly useful form: one minister had conceived of selling used ectoplasmic substance to glue manufacturers, who could tube it up and market it as a cement of unequaled adhesive power. The accident toll had been very high, so the project had been forcibly discontinued. The Ministry had to get used to the idea that far from being a source of extra income for the state, disposing of used dreams would remain one of its duties and expenditures.

David could perfectly recall the shameful and laughable superglue debacle. Millions of little red tubes had flooded store shelves. DIY types had rubbed their hands with glee: finally, a truly adhesive glue capable of resisting any amount of tension, which definitively bonded the most varied materials. The pretty red tubes were a pleasure to purchase because they replaced every type of existing sealant. The euphoria hadn't lasted long. Soon EMTs were dashing to all four corners of the country to try to free foolhardy home improvers from being held hostage by walls, pipes, and roof beams. Faced with the horrifying resistance of the gunk, they'd had to bring themselves to amputate a few fingers, carving deeply into flesh—which had resulted in countless lawsuits. David had long kept one of the scarlet tubes in a desk drawer—not to use, of course, but because he saw it as the strangely iconoclastic coffin of a defunct work of art.

The garbagemen had opened the incubator. With gloved hands, Pit seized the dream slumped like a dead jellyfish and dropped it into his bag. The ectoplasm landed with a flabby smack, leaving just a trace of mucus on the technician's gloves. An official copied the specimen number onto the blank label affixed to the circlip of the tear-proof bag.

"Correct?" he asked, raising a gloomy eye at David.

"Correct," the young man agreed.

The garbagemen did the same for the other dreams that had died as a result of quarantine. David felt a tightness in his throat. He tried to imagine the ordeal the little ectoplasm must have endured just a few days ago. What had they put it through, what kind of idiotic, pseudoscientific torture? They said some lab techs got off on injecting young dreams with a solution of frightfully strong black coffee, that they put still-fragile ectoplasms in special chambers where the unbearable beeping of a digital alarm clock rang out nonstop. All this, in the name of testing the object's physical resistance to outside reality. Was there an ounce of actual science in these routines, or did madness reign, an undisputed sovereign, within the service?

"OK," said Pit Van Larsen. "Here we go." As he passed David, he asked, "You coming all the way or have you had enough?"

"All the way," said the young man softly.

Pit spat on the floor. "Masochist," he said, heading up the line. The garbagemen fell in behind in orderly fashion, each holding at the end of an arm a bag containing the cadaver of a poisoned dream. Their rubber jumpsuits made curious sucking sounds, and David reflected that they must have been sweating atrociously inside those ridiculous outfits.

"See you next time," the fat watchman said as David passed by. There was no malice in it, just the remark of a blasé man who'd finally realized that no matter what you did, everything went pear-shaped.

The garbage truck for dreams was waiting outside, a huge black machine with riveted sides. The bags were carefully deposited in airtight containers to avoid any chance of their exploding in transport. David sat down beside Pit while the others gathered in back for a coffee break. "So," the former dreamer began, "you still in the game? You pulling down a living? That tadpole I wrapped up earlier wasn't about to make you a millionaire. Me, I was making even scrawnier ones toward the end there. I called 'em sleep shits."

"Don't you dream at all anymore?" David inquired, kicking himself for asking the question.

"No," said Pit in a tone of false relief. "They gave me a shot, and ever since then, I don't dive. I dream, but like everyone else— unimportant bullshit you forget as soon as you open your eyes."

He paused for a moment, steering the truck around a bend, then added, "You should do what I did before it's too late. You check out the Ministry's figures lately? You know what the life expectancy is for dreamers? Not so hot. When you start getting old, the ecto-plasms start thickening up; they stay in the lungs and choke you."

"I know," David cut him off sharply. "Skip the lesson." He hesitated, bit his tongue, then ventured, "How does it feel, never seeing the people down there anymore?"

Pit shrugged, but his great gloved hands squeaked on the wheel when he tightened his grip. "I try not to think about it," he whispered. "Anyway, the injection must've killed them. I tell my-self it's like a sick dog, you put it down for its own good. Nothing good can come from hanging out with them. Plus, I felt like I was cheating on my wife with the girl down there, it was ugly."

Not another word was exchanged until they reached the gates of cold storage. That was where they kept the dreams on ice, for lack of a better solution. To keep them from crumbling in the wind or fermenting in their special bins and then exploding, they were frozen. Only freezing allowed them to be kept in a stable form without danger to the environment. Every time he entered the massive labyrinth of cold storage, David was captivated by the ice crystals that drafts swept about like whirlwinds of an endless ice storm. You had to wear protection if you didn't want your ears and cheeks sheared off, and the men who worked in the aisles were all decked out in thick black headgear that made them look like polar explorers. David and the garbagemen got out of the truck and ran to put on thermal jumpsuits in a heated airlock. For the garbagemen, it was always an unpleasant ordeal to extricate themselves from their sweat-slicked black rubber diving suits, towel off in a hurry, and then go to face an underground winter. David stepped out first, his hood drawn down tight in an attempt to ward off the sting of ice shards. The parka was too big, and he tugged furiously on the cord around his waist. His breath exploded in a thick cloud, concealing his view of the maze of stingily lit tunnels. Pit went ahead of him, stooping, followed by his men. They were all clearly in a hurry to have it over with. Their fat antiskid shoes gave the burial an oddly military air. David let himself be guided along. His lips were already frozen. The cold drilled pain into his metal fillings. At last, they reached the door of the freezer room. A crust of ice had formed on the handle, and Pit had some difficulty getting it to turn. Inside, the dreams lay piled in a great heap, a shapeless bric-a-brac of jellyfish petrified by the polar temperatures. Like marble, David thought instinctively, but that wasn't it, not exactly. Marble didn't have the luminescence of ice crystals. The solidified dreams seemed to be dusted with ground diamonds; they lay piled in a great heap, unidentifiable beneath a thick crust of ice. A cemetery, a cemetery of paralyzed ghosts, reduced to the immobility of eternal incarceration. But it was the only way to halt their death throes and the pollution that ensued. Freezing them kept their cadavers from falling apart any further.

"Someday they won't know where to put them anymore," Pit grumbled. "They'll have to stuff 'em in rockets and send them to the stars. They'll put a 'No Vacancy' sign here, like everywhere else."

With a flick of his wrist, he sent the bag's circlip flying and tossed the dead ectoplasm on the crust of ice covering the floor. The dream adhered to it with a clearly audible crackle, and suddenly its color changed. The other garbagemen were already falling back, fleeing the unbearable cold that came in waves from the depths of the room. Pit grabbed David by the arm and pulled him back.

"What are you waiting for?" he growled. "You want your lungs burned? You can't stay here without a mask."

David let himself be led away. He knew full well that the Ministry had been forced to install a nuclear plant at the edge of town for the sole purpose of providing enough energy for the cold storage depots scattered underground. The wintry coffin of dreams required a great deal of power; no one dared think of what might happen if all the funerary freezers suddenly stopped working someday.

"They'd blow up," Pit had replied once, when David asked. "Dream decay is accompanied by intense gas production, which, in such an event, would automatically find itself under pressure. No one knows how long the chambers can hold back the gas. Plus, there's the risk of suffocation, explosion . . ."

True, it was a hell of a headache and no one wanted to think about it too much for now; they'd have to deal with it sooner or later. As usual, not until disaster became imminent. David shed his outfit in the heated airlock and took his leave of Pit. The cold from underground clung to his clothes, and he had a hard time warming back up, even once he was aboveground. He walked quickly, keeping to the sunny sidewalks. Marianne's threats ran through his mind. A rest cure? The road to dismissal always began with a rest cure in an institution full of worn-out, unprofitable dreamers. When the stay was over, you had the right to a second chance, but only one. If that dream ended in failure, you were offered the full discharge injection that Pit Larsen had received. A magic shot that freed you from diving and made you a normal man. Desperately normal.

[10]

The Call of the Deep

He went home, clothes stiff from the underground winter. He could still feel the sting of ice shards on his cheeks, and his chapped lips were bleeding. He made himself some coffee, very sweet, and tried to warm his hands by caressing the mug's porcelain sides. He had his first hallucination as he was walking diagonally across the kitchen. Suddenly it seemed like the tiled floor crumbled beneath his feet, revealing a cleverly concealed liquid expanse. The tiles broke loose, one from the next, sinking into the dark pool that seemed to spread beneath the floor of the entire apartment. David leapt to one side, blinked his eyes. Suddenly, the image vanished. The kitchen floor revealed itself to be untouched. There was no hole, no secret lake . . . He sat down, legs trembling slightly, and passed a hand over his face. The hallucination had been so realistic he'd felt for a split second that he was balancing over a chasm, the tenant of a hut on stilts that was falling to pieces. He wanted another sip of coffee, but was surprised and appalled to find it tasted like seawater. Seaweed floated on the surface of the beverage. In the depths of the mug, sugar had been replaced with silt. He knew instinctively that if he kept staring stubbornly at the mug, he'd soon see fish swimming around the spoon. He closed his eyes, covered his face with his hand. The smell of salt and mud blossomed from the coffeepot's spout, filling the room. He forced himself to breathe slowly. He knew these symptoms perfectly; they always came before a few hours of oneiric trance. It was an alarm signal his unconscious sent out to announce a deep dive. Normally, he would've jumped on the phone and called Marianne to alert her he was about to sink into the coma of dream. She'd have come over right away with her little suitcase, her bottles of glucose, her IV drips. She would've assisted him while he lost consciousness, seeing to the continued function of his deserted body. He made a motion to rise, but changed his mind immediately. No, he shouldn't. If he told her he was about to go under, she'd rush to bring him an inhibitory injection.

"It's for your own good," she would explain in her forbearing nurse's voice. "There's no point tiring yourself since we've suspended you for now." She'd nip the dream in the bud with a squirt of poison, and he wouldn't be able to do a thing to thwart the spread of venom in his body.

He took a deep breath to banish the ball of worry forming at the tip of his sternum. What he was about to do infringed upon the fundamental safety rules of diving, but he couldn't help it, he wanted to see Nadia again too much. Gently, he opened his eyes. The hallucination had worn off. The mug held only cold coffee now. The tiled floor was intact and afforded no glimpse of secret seas ingeniously hidden away. *It's too soon*, the voice of reason murmured to him. *You're still too weak to try another descent, you haven't recovered yet.* But this cautionary advice fell on deaf ears. He got to his feet. The apartment was pitching a bit, like a ship on a rising sea. The objects on the sideboards, the mantles, came and went, obeying the movements of the swell. The entire building was taking to the ocean, slicing through the tide with its redbrick prow. David could clearly hear the regular slap of waves against the walls of the ground floor. He knew that if he opened the curtains, he would see sea foam streaming down the windowpanes. The dive was always heralded by a profusion of maritime hallucinations whose origin he could not explain. He almost lost his balance going down the hallway. Here, there, everywhere, chairs were falling over, dishes slid about in the cupboards, books tumbled from the shelves. They'd left the port; now the apartment building was braving the first breakers of the high seas. Used to it as he was, David still felt overtaken by a slight nausea. He staggered toward the bathroom. The faucets of the sink and tub had turned themselves on, pouring out green, frothy water that smelled of iodine. Gray fish flopped about in the toilet, slapping the porcelain with their powerful fins. David felt his head spin, felt fear knot his stomach. The illusion was too strong. The terribly convincing, almost palpable images presaged a dive of great depth. It was one of those dizzying descents from which he might well never return. If he gave into the trance, he could easily sleep for two weeks, maybe more. Without medical assistance, an escapade like that was tantamount to suicide. In a few days, he would become dehydrated, then slide into a coma. More than one diver had died that way, from an infringement of safety regulations. Diving alone was throwing yourself down a well with a stone tied around your neck. He had to call Marianne. He had to call Marianne so she would come . . . poison the dream.

Seized with vertigo, he dragged himself toward the bedroom and collapsed across the bed like a shipwreck victim clinging to a life raft. The apartment seemed be to hitting twenty-foot troughs, and huge waves came crashing down on the tiled floor with the thunder of a waterfall. The smell of iodine was everywhere now. The salt-starched bedsheets stuck to David's fingers. He tried to remember where he'd hidden the bottles of glucose he'd illicitly acquired. Oh, he could jimmy up a homemade rig that would keep him alive for a while, but none of these pitiful precautions would succeed in keeping the dangers of a deep-sea dive at bay. This time, the call of the deep was terrifying. David felt the apartment warping from the assault of the invisible maelstrom. Soon the floorboards would give way, and he would sink like a rock into the blue waters. He would go deeper than ever before; he could feel it. His feet weighed tons, they would tug him bottomward like the lead ballast of the first undersea explorers. His entire body was becoming heavy, immovable. His limbs would recover their give only once he was submerged. He had to dive, let himself be sucked into the whirlpool.

He was panting, laid out with seasickness. All over the apartment, shelves were emptying their contents, closets were opening, vomiting out plates and saucepans, tables were sauntering from one side of a room to another, scratching the waxed parquet with their hard feet. The building plunged prow-first as if to go under, then abruptly straightened, a castaway who lifts his head above the waves to keep from drowning. David made an effort to sit up. He had to . . . he had to hang the glucose bag from its stand, secure the cannula to the timer that would set them going one after another as the bottles emptied. Enough to hold out for three or four days tops, keeping the rate of flow to a minimum. Would he be back in four days? He had no idea. The deeper you went, the more time it took to come back up; that was one of the fundamental laws of dreaming. The liquid night closed over you, thicker and more restive than the reassuring blue waters of the shallows. There was no point setting any ordinary mechanical device to wake yourself. Bell, beep, alarm, sensory stimulation— nothing worked. A thousand clocks chiming in chorus above the bed of a dreamer in a trance would have deployed their din in vain. David himself had tried it once. The biggest old-fashioned double bell windups, the strident whine of the latest clock radios, had never managed to so much as pierce the shell of dream. The trance insulated you from the world, enveloping you in its sound-proofed carapace. Someone could fire a cannon at the foot of your bed, brand you with a hot iron, and you still wouldn't open your eyes. Marianne had submitted him to all sorts of tests, even going so far to stick needles in the palms of his hands, without ever managing to speed up the ascent. Dreamers remained totally cut off from the outside world, indifferent to their mortal coils, disconnected from their flesh. Waking could only happen from within, when its time came, when the logic of the dream prompted it. For all these reasons, it was suicidal to dive without medical assistance. Though the nurse could in no way come fetch you from deep inside the dream, she was at least in a position to feed your body and keep it from getting dehydrated.

David let himself slip into his bed and crawled toward the closet where he hid his bottles. Would he be strong enough to set them up? Wouldn't the storm snap the mast and shatter the bottles? Oh, c'mon, that was stupid, the storm existed only in his imagination. It was just an expression of the psychic upheaval that was brewing. He pressed down hard on his eyeballs. The pounding of his heart slowed a bit, the blood beating at his temples subsided. He seized upon the momentary calm to raise the metallic mast, hang the bags, lay out the valves and lines. He wondered, with a certain fear, if he would manage to set up the drip without too much damage. He'd always been a fumblefingers. The building was rolling less, but water seemed to be lapping behind the walls and beneath the floorboards, sealing him in the heart of a liquid prison. He sat down in the middle of the bed and rubbed his shoulders; he was cold, yet sweating all over. Water splashed behind the wallpaper with a thick liquid sloshing; he could hear it trickling under the carpet in an unending drainlike gurgle. It occurred to David that people trapped on a sinking ship must feel something similar when the gutted vessel slipped under the surface and pressure forced the last air pockets from the carcass. Marianne . . . should he call Marianne? He was afraid of what awaited him down below, but he was even more afraid of ending up a garbageman with a paralyzed brain.

Slowly, he undressed, tearing off his clothes like remnants of an old skin after molting. With one trembling hand, he tore open the sterile pouch with the IV needle and its transparent little tube. Had he set the timer correctly? His vision blurred and the digits on the counter danced a saraband around the buttons. He quickly arranged the lines, plugged the device in, and stuck the needle in the hollow of his arm. It hurt. He tore off some surgical tape with his teeth, slapped it flat over the insertion point, and lay down on his back. He was nauseous, and his visual acuity was decreasing with each passing second as if night were flooding the apartment. At this simple sign, he knew he was already going down. *This is madness*, he thought with a desperate start, *I should've alerted Marianne, I can still get up, grab the phone* . . . But in reality, he didn't want to. This would be his greatest dive, he could feel it: a journey to the heart of the abyss, into the black hole of the great deep, where he had never before set foot. Where maybe no one, apart from Soler Mahus, had ever set foot. He was going to sink like a stone, let the weight of his rancor drag him down, his fear of being crippled and put out to pasture, all the sadness of murdered dreams. He was going straight to the bottom, cleaving the ocean depths like a diver caparisoned in brass and lead, his gleaming helmet tracing through the liquid night a wake of humming bubbles. *I'm coming!* he thought, closing his eyes. The pillow lapped at his neck, the froth of the sheets licked his loins. He sank and nothing could keep him at the surface anymore.

Suddenly, everything was blue.

[11]

The Basement of the Deep

Jorgo's motorcycles gleamed in the shadows of the garage, show-ing off their tailpipes like strange chrome sculptures. David glimpsed their distressing luster through half-closed eyes. He didn't want to move; his body still seemed too fragile to him. He was afraid that if he got up on one elbow, he'd see his flesh tear away, his bones perforate his epidermis. He was like one of those desserts that had to be left to cool until it reached a certain con-sistency. Sprawled on his stomach, he waited, convinced that if he tried to sit up, his organs would be jostled loose like overripe fruit, landing pell-mell in a horrifying organic mush. Yes, he had to wait, wait for his flesh to firm up, for all the seams and sutures of his internal mechanism to set. At the moment he felt flaccid, fragile, unstable. Bizarre phobias flashed through him: fear his fingers would come off if he grabbed something, fear his toes would scatter if he set foot on the ground. Fear he'd swallow his teeth if he tried to speak . . .

He lay on his belly, against Nadia. He couldn't see the young woman's face because his head was turned the other way, but he knew it was her. They lay entwined, naked and damp in an army-issue sleeping bag, a kind of fat khaki caterpillar. Two bags, in fact, joined by their zippers. He moved his hand slightly, caressing the curve of a hip. Had they made love? He always woke up too late, once the act was over, never retaining any image of their presumed romp. This lacuna frustrated him horribly. But maybe he'd just materialized in Nadia's bag while she was sleeping? His memory was never very clear. It was dark in the garage. Drafts bore odors of grease and gasoline. David shifted his arm to check the depth gauge on his wrist. He shivered at the sight of the reading: *66,000 feet*. Too far down! He'd tumbled to the bottom of a chasm. The pressure here must be terrifying. As for the ascent—that would take an eternity. Nadia's touch dispelled his fears. He wanted to turn around, take her in his arms, but something forced him to get out of the sleeping bag and take a look around. An old survival instinct that admitted no laxness. With infinite precaution, he sat up, expecting to fall to pieces at any minute. It was too early; he wasn't completely reformed yet. He was going to lose an arm, a leg . . . He put a hand on Nadia's shoulder. The flesh was silky but different from human skin, had a radically foreign feel. It reminded him of rubber . . . but *living* rubber. Absurd, but it was the exact sensation beneath his fingertips. Nadia's hair was like artificial fur . . . but again, artificial fur that was somehow alive. David was utterly incapable of explaining these paradoxes;

all he could do was notice them, and be surprised. The way she was, the young thief still seemed more solid than her sisters on the surface, protected from the usual afflictions of the fairer sex. Tenderly, David traced the curve of her shoulder, crossing her chest, letting his finger run all the way to the tip of her breast. Nadia was asleep. Did she dream? No, there was no way, dreaming was a disease that held no sway in the world below. Gently, David drew away and dragged himself from the sleeping bag. He wasn't cold. At his wrist, the big scarlet digits of the depth gauge pulsed like an alarm. He took a few steps among the motorcycles. A bit farther off, Jorgo was sleeping, rolled up in a sleeping bag spattered with old grease. Making contact again was an immutable ritual that always took place according to the same script: David would wake first in a world sleep had vanquished, an anesthetized world where nothing moved. He'd run to the window every time, to try to catch a stray dog pissing against a lamppost, an early bird crossing the sky, but no . . . everything was asleep: dogs, birds, and streetlamps. It was as if everything had stopped while he was away, as if the stilled carousel were gathering dust under its tarp, letting rust slowly devour its gears. As if the traveling fair had closed its doors, deprived of its only customer. It emerged from its torpor only slowly, very slowly, with great pain and creaking, as David's presence gradually relit its bulbs and circuits. The young man walked to the edge of the garage. He was naked, but did not shiver. Here, his body was more impressive, sheathed in hard muscle that made for an excellent defense against the cold. He surveyed the horizon beyond the unused lot. Everything seemed flat, painted on muslin by a bad set dresser. The buildings, the cranes, the former water tank. A two-dimensional image. No doubt it'd get better as the day went on.

He took a few steps out into the litter-strewn field that spread before him to try to convince himself the landscape actually had depth and wasn't merely a painted backdrop. He felt like sticking out his hand to gauge the distance to the horizon, but held back abruptly from fear. What if his fingers stopped dead at the side of that building under construction that only *seemed* to stand two hundred yards away?

He lifted his nose to examine the unmoving clouds, suspended over his head. Wasn't that a bird up there? A bird inexplicably frozen in midair, as if pinned to the sky?

He frowned. The clouds began to move, the bird to flap its wings. The great machinery of the world cranked laboriously into motion again, squeaking and sputtering as it got under way. The cloud mass advanced in fits and start, the bird darted jerkily, as if their movements were controlled by twitchy, ill-oiled machinery. The world of dreams took up its slow rotation again: in a minute the wind would start blowing; the stiffened grass with its paralyzed spine would recover its suppleness. David blinked several times. Perspective came into its own again, the deserted lot stretched out, the horizon line grew distant. He no longer had the unpleasant sensation of standing in museum gallery with his nose a few inches away from a giant painting. The image deepened before his eyes to give him the possibility of entering it. He swallowed. His ears ached, and with the slightest gesture, blood beat painfully at his temples. Too low, he'd gone too low. Would the world of the dream be able to withstand the terrifying water pressure? He felt a painful sensation of heaviness on his shoulders, as if an invisible hammer sought to drive him into the ground. He checked the watch, where the digits were pulsing. Christ! He'd dropped through the seas like an anvil dropped from among the stars. He'd never thought he could pull off such a feat. Had Soler Mahus ever known such terrifying exhilaration? The exhilaration of diving deeper than anyone else?

The sky gave a creak and he shuddered. The water pressure on the vault of the sky must have been nearing the breaking point. The world of the dream was now only a submarine in freefall, a vessel ceaselessly dropping ever lower, whose metal hull the depths had begun to crumple, bringing their force to bear on the fragile stitching of bolts that kept the sheets of armor plating in place.

The sky had groaned; the clouds too. A complaint of abused and twisted metal. David scanned the azure, suddenly convinced a leak would spring open among the clouds, pouring torrents of salt water on the plain. He made an effort to wrest back control of his imagination, well aware that his fears directly affected the organic structure of the oneiric world. It behooved him to remain calm and keep his phobias in check.

He went back into the garage and lit the camp stove, which lay among the tools on the workbench, to make coffee. Now that the wind was working again, he was a bit cold. He sat down, waiting for the water in the saucepan to start simmering. Out the open window sprawled the landscape, the buildings oddly bulbous, a bit squashed on top, as if something were weighing on the upper floors of houses, warping the parallels of walls. Pressure. Still pressure. It mashed objects down, giving them a squat, swollen look. Trees and streetlights stooped, suffering from the invisible hammering. A compressed dog came out from between two abandoned cars. Its abnormal morphology caught David's eye. Its firmly tamped body came down to a kind of hirsute cube that flapped two pairs of tiny paws. The animal's anatomy had been undeniably compacted. Unable to spread out in some harmonious fashion, it had shriveled until it began to look like a figurine of fresh clay flattened by a dissatisfied sculptor's fist. David drew a sharp breath and stared at the creature. After a moment, it seemed that the animal *unfolded*, recovering its natural proportions. Its ears stood up on its head, its paws stretched out . . . The young man tsked in irritation. He could tell it'd take some fine-tuning to compensate for the effect of the great deep. Even the horizon betrayed an exaggerated, completely implausible curvature. All this was very annoying. He inspected the sky again. At least the birds were flying normally; the clouds no longer came to a sudden stop and crashed into each other like carriages on a train that had braked too abruptly.

He reckoned he had set things straight enough to wake his companions. He grabbed the saucepan and poured the water slowly over the grounds filling the paper filter. He was a bit afraid of seeing Nadia emerge from the sleeping bag with a misshapen, cuboid body, her legs crooked, her breasts square. He'd never dragged them this far down before, to these unfathomable depths, the hunting ground of great dreamers. How would they take the submersion? The smell of coffee spread through the air, supplanting that of gasoline. Nadia stirred, then Jorgo. Their awakenings were always difficult, mechanical, their gestures horrendously approximate. Whenever they came out of sleep, it was like they needed to learn to stand again, to walk, to speak. They were like babies with only a few minutes to learn everything. However brief, these moments were extremely painful for David, who felt each time like he was seeing cardboard dummies or lobotomized simpletons come to life. He decided to let the aroma of the coffee do its work and left to get dressed. His clothes had been tossed in a heap on the suitcase of brushed steel he was never without in the world of the dream. He knelt and undid the clasps. The armored luggage contained quite an assortment of drugs whose vials were lined up like strange ammo on a sheet of black rubber, held in place by leather loops. There were concentrated rationality pills, logic tablets, plausibility adjustment drops. And above all, an array of fast-acting tone powders that allowed him to instantly modulate the nuance of a moment: irony powder, comedy powder, distancing powder, which when snorted off the back of your hand immediately attenuated the excessively tragic outline of any situation. Used wisely, these chemical tools enabled skillful corrections over the course of a story, slowing the formation of nightmare and its inevitable corollary: ejection into reality.

David gently stroked the vials. With these drugs, he had no need for a noisy, cumbersome sidearm. All he had to do was know how to juggle the pills, know which capsule to swallow at the right moment.

When he was done dressing, he saw that Nadia and Jorgo had taken up seats on either side of the workbench and were drinking their coffee in silence. They were staring into space, and feeling around a bit with their cups to find their mouths, but apart from these details, everything was going well; their bodies had suffered no visible alterations. David sat down at one end of the table and watched them. In fact, he knew nothing about them. Who was Nadia? Who was Jorgo? He'd racked his brains, but couldn't manage to dredge up from memory the slightest snatch of information about their pasts, their childhoods . . . And yet if he'd created them from scratch, as Marianne claimed, he should've known all the most intimate secrets buried in the depths of their skulls. He should've enjoyed the omniscient view of novelists for whom characters were completely transparent, from whom they could hide nothing. In that case, why were Nadia and Jorgo sitting in front of him like opaque, taciturn, and mysterious figures?

"They don't exist," Marianne had told him time and again. "They're just images of your own self. Symbolic puppets that each represent an impulse, a tendency, a complex, a facet of your individuality. They have no depth because they're not really alive." But David had never been able to accept this line of reasoning. Nadia lived a real life. He was sure, now that the world of dream was back in working order, that the young woman's skin had lost its rubbery feel and turned into warm, actual flesh. Couldn't he spot, at this very moment, the bluish tracery of veins beneath the milky skin of her arms?

"It'll be a big score this time," he declared after clearing his throat. "No jewelry boutiques. Something huge. A world-famous masterpiece."

The words had formed themselves independently of his will. They'd left his mouth without his even knowing and flown to meet his companions. Where had they come from, these plans he hadn't known a thing about a minute earlier? Nadia and Jorgo turned toward him, frowning.

"You sure we're up to that?" Nadia fretted. "A jewelry boutique is one thing. A museum is something else altogether."

"Aiming kind of high, aren't you?" Jorgo chimed in. "I mean, we're just small-timers. Why try to be the all-stars of the heist world? Our haul doesn't do it for you anymore? You already blow everything we got off the diamonds from the last job?"

David shrugged. He'd never managed to make them understand that once in the real world, the loot from the jewelry stores no longer retained its original shape. Despite all his explanations, they stubbornly persisted in believing that the diamonds from dreams became real diamonds when you woke up. When he'd confessed that the fruit of their theft materialized as soothing knickknacks that were sold for a trifle, they'd burst out laughing, convinced he was joking. He hadn't dared insist, for fear he'd go down in their esteem. How could the head of a gang be content with living the life of a pathetic government art worker in the surface world when they imagined him spending his days in golden palaces and casinos?

"My credibility's at stake," he lied. "I need a big score to get back in the game. The diamonds I brought back the other day were fake."

Nadia swallowed hard, which made her naked breasts shake. David happily breathed in the redhead's familiar scent. If she'd started sweating, that meant she was done taking shape. She wasn't rubber and nylon anymore, but well and truly flesh and hair; it didn't matter that he knew nothing about her. Besides, did you ever really know anything about the people around you? In his everyday life, David most often felt like he was rubbing shoulders with robots devoid of the slightest scrap of humanity.

"A museum, that's big-time," Jorgo muttered. "What do you want to take?"

"A ten-foot-by-six-foot painting," David heard himself reply. "*The Battle of Kanstädt*." And he slid toward them a catalog of paintings, which had mysteriously appeared in his hands. They bent over the workbench to examine the reproduction. He felt their hair touch his. *What the hell is happening to me?* David thought. *I'm losing my head. It's the rapture of the deep. Past sixty thousand feet, you become a megalomaniac. Like Soler Mahus and his white creatures, his mythic animals, his unicorns and yetis.*

He was afraid. At that very moment the sky let out the groan of a chassis compressed beyond its limits. Pressure. The pressure was there, weighing on the clouds, the roof of the garage. Even the flame on the camp stove was bizarrely flattened. The image of a submarine crushed by the depths leapt to mind again. He saw the submersible crumple into itself like a beer can, scrunch up in a terrible screech of sheet metal. What if the ocean closed up on them, crushing the world of the dream?

The sky wasn't as blue as usual, and behind its fragile layer the enormous mass of black water could be felt, waters no light had ever pierced, where even the fish proved to be blind. David closed his eyes. Would his sixth sense be up to detecting any possible leak and plugging it? Nadia and Jorgo were talking, but he wasn't listening. Their eyes shone with a strange greed; their mouths too, as if they fed on David's presence, as if they were stuffing themselves on his lifeblood, stealing hunks of flesh from him to increase their own density. Vampires, the young man thought, stiffening against a fleeting reaction of disgust. One day, if he was so careless as to linger in the depths of dream, would his dear companions give into the temptation to devour him, to live at his expense? No, of course not, he was losing his mind, he had nothing to fear from Nadia and Jorgo.

And yet their eyes, like IV needles . . .

He shook himself, banishing the phantasmagoria of the rapture of the deep. While Nadia reviewed the various difficulties of the job, David's mind flew off, left the garage for an inspection of the heavenly vault. There, between those clouds over there— was that a bird, or a crack? Astride the wind, he examined the world the way a sailor would the hold of a ship, lantern raised, to be sure that the hull showed no signs of leakage. He was sitting at the table, drawing up plans, determining precise timing, and at the same time he was roaming the world below, palpating the heavens, tasting water from the fountains to make sure the seas weren't trying to infiltrate the dream. Things like that often happened down here. Moments ran parallel, time shrank or expanded. Parentheses opened in the fabric of events. Time leapt from morning to night in the blink of an eye. Nothing here worked like it did up above.

"This is a really big job," Nadia murmured. "You know the whole museum's under surveillance, right? Electric eyes that set off alarms at the first sign of movement? They sweep the rooms nonstop and can spot a mouse at thirty yards."

David nodded. He recognized the speech, straight out of a crime novel he'd read as a kid, whose plot he'd entirely forgotten. He was willing to bet the name of the painting he'd mentioned earlier, *The Battle of Kanstädt*, came from the same book.

"We need a specialist," Nadia said, serious. "Only Professor Zenios can neutralize the electric eyes. He's a hypnotist. When he's through with them, all the sensors will be able to see is what he wants them to."

David was delighted. He'd never heard of this Zenios before. Wasn't that added proof of the autonomy of the world below? He wasn't the one who made up all the characters. They existed outside himself, had their own lives which owed him nothing, or just about.

"Let's go with Zenios," he said. As a child, he'd habitually relished chapters that detailed the preparations for a heist. He adored the lists of objects, the blueprints, the special outfits, the ingenious tools that came into play. Today he kept back, out of step with the others, cheated of his pleasure. He eyed Nadia with a sudden desire to grab a pin and stab one of her breasts to see the blood flow . . . more exactly, *to make sure she could bleed*. Marianne's poisonous rationality was inside him; though he'd plugged his ears, something from her damned speeches had slipped through. An interpretive virus that risked perturbing him during the heist—NO! Nadia was no symbol, Jorgo either. They weren't puppets, paper cutouts a mere breeze could carry off, THEY WERE REAL. Nadia smelled of sleep and sweat, and Jorgo grime and grease.

Suddenly, the young woman grabbed his wrist. Her eyes opened wide when she saw the figure on the depth gauge.

"You're crazy," she gasped. "No one's ever gone this far down before. We're not equipped for missions this deep into the abyss. Are you trying to kill us?"

"The sooner it's over, the sooner we'll go back up," David murmured. "I know I'm putting our world in danger, but if I don't bring back anything they won't let me dive anymore, see? This is my last chance. I have to prove to them I can pull off something as well as Soler Mahus. If I resurface empty-handed, they'll poison you, the sky will rot, the houses crumble, and soon you'll be nothing but a porcelain tumor deep in my head. A tumor that will make me deaf, dumb, and a vegetable."

He fell silent, out of breath. Nadia put her hand on his. It was warm and moist, like a real hand.

[12]

Faces from the Antipodes

They met up with Zenios the next . . . day? Zenios was a little fellow stuffed into a black raincoat, with a hat so big for his head that it almost covered his eyebrows. A gray goatee and round steel-rimmed glasses hid what remained of his face. He spoke with a strong Russian accent and claimed he was capable of hypnotizing anything with a glass lens on it, from screens to electric eyes. He performed a demonstration with the help of a portable television, which he mesmerized right in the middle of a maudlin soap opera and "persuaded," with a few bizarrely whispered phrases, to display the first three hundred columns of the telephone book.

While the names and figure skipped across the screen, he declared in magisterial tones, "The duration of the trance depends, of course, on the quality of the object. The more sophisticated the object, the more limited the effects of persuasion. A television is an easy target, but the security system in a museum is much more recalcitrant. I will hypnotize the sensors, affirm that all they are seeing is a succession of empty rooms, but this suggestion won't last more than half an hour. Little by little, the electronic circuits will emerge from their stupor and become aware of reality. If you're still on the premises then, they'll set off the alarm, and I will be unable to help you . . ."

They met up with Zenios the next day (or a few minutes later). He was a little fellow squeezed into a black raincoat, with a hat . . . they met . . . David was having the hardest time keeping track of dream time. Sudden lapses denied him the action's linear progression. He would emerge from sleep right in the middle of a conversation or meeting like a sleepwalker who'd just fallen out a window and woken up in midair.

"You're distracted," Nadia told him. "Sometimes I feel like you're growing transparent, fading away. What's on your mind?"

"My body," the young man confessed. "I left it up there, unmonitored. It's the first time, see? No one knows I'm here, and I can't figure out how long I've been gone. If something happens to it up there—"

Nadia frowned. No one, indeed, knew how time down below compared to time on the surface. The flow of time in the dream world seemed to proceed by fits and starts. Sometimes gestures stretched out endlessly like in a slow-motion scene, and at other times, it all went by very fast. Actions fled by, sped up, while conversations became an incomprehensible chirping. David wondered if the temporal flux wasn't governed by purely subjective criteria, the mind condensing painful or boring moments in order to protract pleasant ones instead, dragging them out until they were a kind of amber where you wound up getting trapped. It was just a theory, but he knew an hour of dream didn't equal an hour of reality; the exchange rate was much more complex.

"I'm worried, because an hour here is almost a day up there," he explained clumsily. "Up top they think it's the other way around, but they're wrong."

"Makes sense," the young woman remarked. "Down here you live life to the fullest, while up there your life is empty, worthless. You need a lot of real time to buy just a minute of dreams."

"Yeah," David admitted, "but right now my body's all alone. When the glucose bottles run out, it'll start to die."

"You worry too much about it," Nadia said with a trace of aggression. "It's just a vehicle. Your mind isn't up there, it's down here."

"But if my flesh and blood body dies," David stammered, "will we go on living? I mean: what if we need it, like a plant needs the soil in its pot?"

"No," the young woman hissed, "that's just a superstition. We have an independent existence. If your body died you'd stay here forever, with us. You wouldn't lead the double life of a traveling salesman anymore: one day here, the next at the antipodes . . ."

There was a hint of reproach in her voice, as if she suspected David of leading a hidden life in reality, from which he derived ineffable pleasures. As if the body he went on and on about was but an excuse for escapades. The life of a traveling salesman? The accusation stirred an echo of vague memories in him, blurry images involving the antipodes . . . He gave up. The plant metaphor obsessed him. His body was the nourishing earth the dream world depended on; if that earth turned to sterile ash, they would all die. The withering of his flesh would undoubtedly lead to the necrosis of the oneiric world; they were all linked, Siamese, inseparable, unable to live one without the other. What would happen to him if he never went back up? If he *deserted*? First the sky would fade away, he thought. Little by little, the sun would lose its heat. Objects would become transparent as jellyfish; our hands would pass through them when we tried to grab them.

"Stop indulging your fears!" Nadia flared. "You'll summon the nightmare. Is that what you want? Complete disaster?"

"Of course not," he said, and went to the window to make sure the world was still stable and no symptoms betrayed the formation of an embryonic cataclysm. Except for a slight warping from the pressure, he noticed nothing, but he was still nervous. He didn't like arguing with Nadia about his double life in the real world. He'd tried to tell her before just how boring that life was, but she remained obsessed by the women he associated with up there.

"That Marianne," she'd hiss wrathfully. "She coddles you like a nursemaid. And then there's that Antonine you're sleeping with—"

"But that doesn't count," David whined. "Up there I'm

pathetic, ugly. You wouldn't even recognize me. My face, my body are very different from the ones I use down here. I'm just a very average guy. You've got no reason to be jealous. That's someone else up there, living that life. A loser."

"I'm sure you're exaggerating," Nadia grumbled. "You can't change that much just by surfacing. Besides, you're bringing back all that loot. You're rich. Women like that."

The more concrete details he gave her about his everyday life, the more unbelievable it seemed to her. *Come on!* He'd try harder. *Life up there can't be that dull, that devoid of appeal.* These conversations made David ill at ease. He was often tempted to fast-forward through them, but each time he tried, Nadia would interrupt his attempt and reestablish a slower pace, one more conducive to discussion. How many days since he'd passed out on the bed, the glucose drip stuck in his arm?

"You're always looking for reasons to leave again," Nadia grumbled. "You come here, but you keep thinking about what's going on up there, while you're away. If you really loved us, you wouldn't give a damn what happens to your body."

Maybe she was right, but he couldn't let it go, and wore himself out on rough calculations in an attempt to pinpoint the temporal exchange rate between reality and dream. He always came up with the same result: the coin of reality was small change down here. It was even unpleasantly like those garishly colored banknotes from banana republics, stately on the fingers but barely enough to buy a pocketful of matches.

"Desert!" Nadia whispered to him deep in the sleeping bag

that . . . night? "They can't come looking for you here. Our borders are impassable. They've got no way of making you come back!"

David silenced her with a kiss. Her mouth was hot. Hotter than a real woman's. And he moved to cover his body with hers and make love.

[13]

The Battle of Kanstädt

Just as he was about to lower himself onto her, he realized they weren't in the sleeping bag anymore. Instead, they were sitting in a parked car in front of the museum esplanade. This kind of temporal short-circuiting was very common in dreams. Whenever he found himself confronted with it, David still felt for a fleeting moment like he was trapped in a falling elevator, and his stomach flipped. Discreetly, he checked that his clothes were on right with one hand. Nadia was driving; she didn't seem to have noticed the temporal splice. David glanced in the rearview mirror. Zenios and Jorgo were sitting in back, silent, staring straight ahead. There was something uncertain about their features, as was often the case with supporting characters. If you weren't careful, their expressions ended up completely erased, their faces settling for standard-issue holes and slits without any personalizing elements.

David squinted to increase the definition. At any rate, he'd never really paid attention to Jorgo, and thought of him more as an amiable idiot.

"Did you take the pills?" Nadia asked in a tense voice. Instinctively, David popped open the steel suitcase on his lap and opened a vial of pills.

"Stay on top of your consistency," Nadia repeated. "But above all, stay cool. You know how paintings are in our world; they're nothing at all like what you have up there. So stay calm, cool, collected."

David tapped a little distancing powder onto the back of his hand. The trick was getting the dose just right.

"I popped a nuclear suppository," Jorgo crowed. "I feel awesome!"

"How deep are we?" Nadia asked, ignoring the interruption.

"Still 66,000," David murmured. "And holding."

He recalled the last time, when he'd let his fantasies get away from him, almost turning the car into a shark. That wasn't going to happen tonight. This time he was fine. The powder had numbed his nostrils, tattooing a cold patch between his eyebrows.

"You're up, Professor," Nadia said, opening the door. They got out of the car and headed across the white esplanade single-file. The night was starless, oppressively dark. No phosphorescent fish crossed the sky. David felt reassured by just how real things felt. The situation was well in hand.

"Don't overdo it," Nadia whispered. Get too rational, and Zenios will lose his powers. A character like him can only exist in a certain dream context."

As usual, she was right; David relaxed his attention slightly. Before them, the museum rose like cliffs of white marble, surrounding them with its frozen, pompous statuary. The stone lions supporting the banister remained inert, as they would have in reality. David felt curiously detached, barely concerned by everything going on. The powder ran along his nerves, dulling the anxiety he'd normally have felt.

"There's the first electronic eye," Zenios whispered, indicating a kind of lens sticking out of the wall. "The whole area around the entrance lies within its field of vision. Nothing can get through the door without its immediately noticing and sounding the alarm. I'll put it to sleep. Plug your ears so you won't hear what I'm saying."

Nadia pulled a tin of wax earplugs out of her pocket and passed them around. Zenios had approached the sensor, taking care to stay outside its range. From the movements of his lips, it was clear he'd begun droning his hypnotic suggestions. It took a while, then the eye began to blink. It teared up, and then its protective metal lid drew down with a squeak. At the same time, the gates opened. David took the plugs from his ears.

"We're in," Zenios sighed. "The eye is asleep. In its dreams, it's still watching the entrance, and all is well. Remember, the hypnotic trance only lasts thirty minutes. If you're out before it wakes up, it won't remember a thing, and won't be able to bring testimony against you."

David nodded and pushed the gate aside. His footsteps echoed in the great glass atrium. The exhibit halls, harshly lit and yet deserted, were somehow unsettling.

"No time to waste," said Nadia, clicking her stopwatch. "Professor, you take out the other three eyes in the main gallery and go on out without us, as planned. Are we good?"

The old man nodded and started immediately for the long exhibit hall on the ground floor. Jorgo was champing at the bit, tools slung across his chest in a bandolier. Nadia put a hand on David's arm, squeezed his biceps.

"Don't forget," she repeated. "Paintings down here aren't just colors splashed on canvas. Try not to be too shocked by what you find. If you panic, you'll destabilize the world, and bring nightmare crashing down on us."

At the other end of the gallery, Zenios was waving them forward with his arm. The second eye was asleep, its metal lid lowered. David tried to situate the painting in the museum. It was, he thought, at the far end of an endless corridor of varnished paintings, in an impasse of a room with no doors leading outside. But his facts remained hazy. *But I was the one who planned this job!* he thought, surprised. Nadia had taken the lead. She advanced with a firm step in her black leather, her face unreadable, sparing of gesture and expression.

"It is done," Zenios announced, joining them. "They're all asleep. Keep an eye on your watches. I'll be waiting in the car."

He walked on tiptoe, as if the floor burned his feet. It seemed he had but one desire: to get out of this mousetrap posthaste. Nadia turned away from him and oriented herself with the map from her pocket.

"Five hundred feet of hallway," she said coolly. "*The Battle of*

Kanstädt's all the way at the back. We'll have to cross the entire length of the museum."

They started walking, forcing themselves not to run, freezing whenever a car passed by the esplanade outside. The parquet let out a terrible creaking beneath their feet, and David wondered if the racket would wind up waking the optical sensors. *A masterpiece,* whispered a voice inside him. *A painting of inestimable value, unique in all the world. You've never stolen anything close to it before.* The Battle of Kanstädt *is your world's equivalent of Soler's white beasts. The symbol of a colossal work . . . as huge as the great dream out there on Bliss Plaza, the one that put an end to the war. If you can bring it back to the surface, you'll be famous overnight.* He passed a hand over his face to check if he was sweating. His skin was dry. Thanks to the distancing powder, fear was turning into a feeling of curiosity and rather pleasant impatience.

They reached the end of the gallery at last. The painting in its heavy gilded frame suddenly seemed as vast and unbudgeable as a building façade. It was a gigantic work executed in a very eighteenth-century style that packed in a mind-boggling hodgepodge of men, cannons, horses, foot soldiers, and cavalry. Smoke from salvos hovered in an acrid layer over the landscape, and entire battalions maneuvered in its shadow. From one side of the frame to the other, thousands of miniature men were busy running, charging, dying, and each of them had been painted with an almost hallucinatory eye for detail. Nothing had been left out: not the bicornes, the buttons on the frock coats, the insignia on the uniforms. Each soldier had a face distinct from that of his companions, entirely his own. And each face reflected a specific emotion: fear, anger, rage, cowardice, despair, exhaustion. It was a fabulous work of truly terrifying mastery. Black-jacketed guardsmen confronted red-jacketed guardsmen in a tumultuous and pitiless contest in the middle of a muddy field that the pounding of artillery had turned into a lunar landscape. All those swords, those pikes, gave off a wounding gleam. A cavalry charge hurtled down a hillside, sending chunks of peat flying; cannonballs tore through the air, fleeing to meet mounts, shattering the breast-plates of riders, scattering heads and limbs in their wake. David blinked, dumbfounded by so much turmoil.

All three of them were breathing hard. The painting was a window onto another world, a well from which rose a fearsome draft that threatened to knock them off their feet at any moment. The frame seemed a rim they didn't dare lean on, for fear it might suddenly crumble. David knelt slowly, praying the parquet wouldn't creak at the touch of his knees. Jorgo had opened his satchel and pulled out a bulging medical kit, which he unrolled on the floor, revealing bottles, vials, and syringes. *How many people were there?* David thought frantically. *How many animals? Hundreds . . . thousands?* Suddenly he realized he'd dreamed too big. Even with all three of them, they'd have a hard time wrapping up in twenty minutes. Nadia had already grabbed a syringe, stuck it into a bottle. Jorgo grabbed a big spray bottle full of topical anesthetic solution and began squirting the painting to numb its skin. But the haze floating over the battlefield tended to catch the fine droplets.

"You sure you want to do this?" Nadia asked, taking a step toward the painting, syringe in hand. "David? We can still go right now, leave all this behind. This is too big for us. It's not going to end well."

His thoughts exactly, but then, bracing himself against his fear, he filled his syringe in turn and moved toward the bottom right corner of the painting. A horse there had been struck by a hail of bullets, its rider toppling backward, futilely brandishing his saber. A handsome bit of painting in which the hooves of the slaughtered animal reared and struck at the smoke in a kind of whirlwind where a few ghostly figures could be glimpsed. The black holes in the man's breastplate clearly indicated that he would be dead before he hit the ground. Foot soldiers were running round the horse, bayonets lowered. Their eyes were closed. The great mêlée boiling over the crucible of the plain pitted companies of somnambulists against each other, whose lethal acts were carried out in the heart of a deep slumber. David leaned forward, looking for generals atop the traditional hillock overlooking the carnage. They were also sleeping, feet in stirrups, only pretending to survey the struggle, and their horses were sleeping too, knees locked in equine fashion. It was as if some enchantment had struck them in mid-action, suspending the flow of time, arresting them in unconsciousness like the courtiers in Sleeping Beauty's castle. Nadia appeared to register no surprise at the spectacle. Leaning on the edge of the tediously ornamented frame, she'd already jabbed a horse in the thigh, injecting a few drops of sedative into the substance of the painting.

"Maintain a light touch," she whispered. "The important

thing is not to wake them up. Watch out—the haze is keeping the local anesthetic from settling in right."

"But—" David stammered. "They're all sleeping! Did you see that? It's incredible—a battle where all the soldiers have their eyes closed! You can't tell until you're right up close to it! It must be some kind of allegory, right?"

"What the hell are you babbling about?" Nadia snapped. "They've got their eyes closed because it's nighttime—time to sleep! Down here paintings need sleep too, just like people. Stop babbling and drug them. If we don't put them all under, they'll wake up with a start as soon as we start moving the painting."

She did not stop inoculating as she spoke. The tip of the syringe came and went like the stinger on some insatiable insect. She pricked horses in the croup, men in the shoulder, devoting only one or two seconds to each. Jorgo was doing the same. He'd tackled the other half of the painting and was working on the enemy army, anesthetizing squadrons on the march, charging horses. When the syringe was empty, he pierced the rubber seal on another bottle and filled it back up.

"They're light sleepers," Nadia whispered, a fine sweat gleaming on her brow. "It's a very old painting, which means it doesn't need much sleep. Plus, the period frame is crippled with rheumatism, which the crossbeams in back can feel. That means the work could wake up at any moment, and in a bad mood. You can imagine the problems that would cause . . ."

David couldn't imagine a thing. He found himself suddenly paralyzed with terror, and the syringe between his fingers began to shake. Finally, he made up his mind to inject the great rearing horse, repeating to himself, *This is madness! Sheer madness!* When the needle sank into a soft, fibrous mass reminiscent of striated muscle, he almost let out a cry of horror. It was as if he'd just injected a real horse. A . . . real? horse, but two-dimensional, and no more than four inches tall.

"Faster!" Nadia panted, "faster!" She was right. Why was he wasting time being astonished? He was in the dream world, and anything was possible. Anything!

"This is a very powerful tranquilizer. Don't use too much," the young woman repeated. "Two drops for horses, one for people—that's enough. Get it right, or you'll poison them. If they die, they'll rot; a black patch will form on the painting's surface and oxidation from decomposition will make a hole in the canvas. If that happens, the painting will be worthless."

David felt his pulse swelling the veins at his temple. Briefly, he tried to imagine the death of a figure in a painting: first the colors fading away, then the bristling blisters of fermenting paint, mushrooms forming beneath the glaze. An ugly little rot that spread like sickness from the foot of a tree and ended up making a person-shaped hole . . .

He jabbed and jabbed, trying to be as fast and efficient as his companions. He was abruptly ashamed to have dragged them into such folly, ashamed of abusing his influence over them. They'd obeyed without protest, like docile slaves, resigned as soldiers who make it a point of honor never to challenge an order. Lost in these thoughts, he jabbed a horse too hard; for a split second, its eye

opened. The flash of white from the painting's surface made David back up a few steps, hair standing up on the back of his neck,
but already the eyelid had closed again.

"Ten minutes," Nadia announced, her voice flat. Empty
bottles of tranquilizer piled up at the foot of the painting. Jorgo
swore. He'd just snapped his needle on a cavalryman's breastplate.
David could no longer see what he was doing. He jabbed, jabbed,
and jabbed away, saturating the canvas even as he tried to control
the force of the plunger. Two drops for animals, one drop for
people . . . but there were so many men, so many horses! And
the dead? The ones lying in the mud, a shattered sword in their
hands? And the animals gutted by bullets? Did he have to drug
them too? Not daring to interrupt Nadia with stupid questions, he
jabbed at random, knocking out the living and the dead alike. The
painting blurred before him. All those tiny bodies in uniform, in
serried ranks, those sleepwalkers halted in the middle of a killing
blow, bayonet brandished, saber raised, not even taking a seat at
night to rest their weary bodies.

In the same emotionless voice, Nadia continued to lay out the
curious rules governing the lives of paintings. "If you see a horse
or a man lie down, it means you've given them too much. They
won't necessarily die, but if they make it, there's no guarantee
they'll take up the exact position they were in before they passed
out. So you understand the scope of what I'm saying: if so much
as one figure, *a single figure*, changes position, we'll find ourselves
with a different painting on our hands—a fake, a copy. If just one
of these soldiers leaves his spot and crawls into a ditch to sleep better, *The Battle of Kanstädt* will no longer match up with pictures

in art history books or museum catalogs. You get me? Make sure none of these soldiers collapses when you pull out your needle. If that happens, try to force them back up by massaging the canvas top to bottom with the tip of your finger. Usually that's enough; reflex kicks in, and they instinctively assume their poses again."

David's head was buzzing. From the nervous sweat moistening his palms, he knew the distancing powder wasn't working anymore. He needed to stop what he was doing and take a pill, but he didn't dare break the rhythm. He couldn't afford the luxury. Still, he feared a nightmare might form and capsize the operation. This was the first time he'd ever mounted a theft of such scope; till now, he'd just been a small-time hoodlum robbing window displays, local jewelry stores. The painting was something else, the guarantee of a magnificent object, a work as powerful as that of Soler Mahus. This time, he wouldn't go back up carrying a mere knickknack doomed to die in quarantine. No container would be big enough to accommodate the product of his dream. The museum would have to take exceptional measures, dispatch all its specialists on the double . . . Marianne could keep her advice, her sermons, and go back to sleeping in her suitcase like a good little boarder. This time, there would be no more doubting his talent; the great dream on Bliss Plaza would be but a bouquet of wilted daisies beside what he was about to snatch from the deep.

"Ow!" The needle had slipped along a saber blade and plunged too deeply into the torso of a standard-bearer with a powder-blackened face. A fraction of a second after pressing on the plunger, David distinctly saw the tiny figure's eye open, burning with rage.

"Five minutes," Nadia announced. A dark rivulet stained her T-shirt between her breasts. Jorgo's face was glistening as if rubbed with oil.

"Quick—we have to take the canvas down," the young woman ordered. "We'll have just enough time to get out of here before the electric eyes come out of their trance."

Jorgo had taken out a razor and began cutting the canvas along the frame. Nadia did the same. The varnish-covered painting resisted the blades.

"David!" the young woman hissed. There's a ladder in the closet. We'll need it to cut across the top of the painting."

David shook himself, dropped the syringe, and turned toward the closet, but it seemed to leap back like a timid animal afraid to be touched. That was a bad sign. Such distortions of perspective signaled the embryonic formation of a nightmare. With a feverish hand, he groped for his drugs. His nerves were crackling like short-circuiting high-tension wires. He took a quick sniff of distancing powder from the back of his hand. The icy burn ravaged his nasal cavity and exploded in his brain, lodging like a harpoon in the middle of his head. The closet door drew obediently closer. He opened it and took out a window washer's stepladder. He went blank, lost some time. When he opened his eyes again, Nadia and Jorgo were laying the giant canvas on the floor.

"To roll it up," the young woman explained, "like a rug." The notion seemed so out of place that David burst out laughing.

"You're starting to take off," Nadia snapped aggressively. "Try to control your dream instead of letting it carry you away!"

She was absolutely right. Besides, he felt calmer already,

cooler. Suddenly, the painting seemed almost ugly to him, without interest. Was it even worth stealing?

Nadia and Jorgo picked up the rolled canvas, each taking an end on one shoulder. With a firm step, they headed up the long hall leading to the exit.

"Two minutes," the young woman whispered dully. David couldn't understand why she was so scared. The things you could get done in two minutes! For instance . . . They were running now, pounding the parquet, filling the building with the rumble of a stampede. Nadia was staring at the electric eye overlooking the entrance. The metal eyelid was rising very slowly, with an interminable creak. With a desperate burst of speed they ran for the exit, tripping over the doorsill and tumbling head over heels down the stairs. The moment they hit the broad slabs of the esplanade, sprawling, the optical sensor raised its protective lid with a sharp click, coming out of its slumber to resume surveillance.

"It worked!" Jorgo exulted. Nadia silenced him with a wave. The canvas had unrolled coming down the stairs, and now lay spread in the middle of the plaza, a great gleaming rug with frayed edges. Puddles from the last shower (when had it rained? David had no memory of it) trickled iridescent water over its surface. David would've liked to know if contact with liquid risked damaging the painting, but not a word came from his mouth. The cold night wind made his teeth chatter, suddenly making him realize his clothes were so soaked he could've wrung sweat from them. The moisture assaulted his nerves, wrecking the powder's effect; he got to his feet, feeling instead like he'd landed heavily on them. Migraine pains went shooting through his skull. He staggered, fought to stay upright while Nadia and Jorgo struggled with the drenched canvas. Nadia was losing her cool, insulting Jorgo in a low voice because he was slow to lift the painting from the puddle where it was steeping.

"Take it easy!" David cried. "The varnish protects the colors. They won't run that easily."

"You don't get it!" the young woman hissed. "The cold water'll wake the soldiers! Jesus Christ! It's like tossing a bucket of water at their faces!"

David rushed forward, not sure he really understood the new danger. Grabbing the canvas by one of its sides, he tried to lift it from the ground. But it was abnormally heavy, and he could make out confused movements on its surface . . . White spots, myriad tiny white spots. Eyes. Thousands of eyes, opening one after the next. Suddenly, those eyes were all he could see, piercing the darkness of the sullied varnish.

"It's the cold water," Nadia panted. "Shit! Shit! Shit! It's cancelled out the tranquilizer. Now they're going to be angry. We'll never get the painting to the car."

David felt the claws of nightmare sink into the flesh of his shoulders. Everything was going off the rails; he could feel it. So close, and yet . . . less than fifty yards lay between them and the car. He wanted to get ahold of the canvas, but it was like grabbing a handful of pincushions. The foot soldiers' bayonets massed at the edge of the painting had just pierced his fingers. A muddled noise rose from the image, whose surface puckered, wrinkled, like living flesh shot through with shivers.

"Out of the way!" Nadia cried, pulling him back. "It's dangerous. They're going to defend themselves!"

But David clung to his loot, determined not to be deprived. He understood her warning only when a tiny cannonball tore through his jacket and whistled by his ear. A cannonball from one of the thousand cannons depicted in the painting. A cannonball about the size of a bullet, which had come less than an inch away from blowing his head off.

"C'mon," Nadia begged, tugging at his sleeve. "It's fucked now. We can't take it anymore. It's that antivandalism treatment they give famous works—it makes them able to defend themselves in case of theft, or attack . . . sometimes even a bad review. It'll shoot at anything that moves, and the noise will bring the cops. C'mon, it's over. We have to run."

David remained frozen, shoulders hunched. Now the salvos were rolling round the esplanade, getting louder with each echo. It was like a firing squad had set up shop right in front of the museum, executing statues and the columns of the peristyle. The cannonballs ricocheted, yowling, while the smell of burnt powder rose from the canvas. Like his companions, David was flattened on the ground, not daring to lift his head. *Nightmare*, he thought. *It ended up happening anyway, even though everything seemed to be going so well.* And why were there puddles of icy water on the esplanade? Had it rained without his knowing . . . or was the vault of the sky beginning to give way beneath the pressure, letting the sea seep into the dream world?

Jorgo had begun crawling toward the car where Professor

Zenios was waving at them desperately. The wail of a police siren burst out from the far end of the avenue. In a few seconds, the flashing lights could be seen . . . David straightened up, teeth clenched, and made one last move for the painting. This time, a cannonball tore through his eyebrow, and his face was drowned in blood.

"We'll come back!" Nadia sobbed against his temple "We'll give it another shot sometime. C'mon! C'mon!"

He let himself be dragged away. They were almost off the esplanade when Jorgo crumpled, a black hole between his shoulder blades. The kid collapsed, mouth open, not even trying to cushion the fall, and lay there without moving.

"Jorgo!" Nadia screamed hysterically. "Jorgo!"

David didn't know what to do. The beelike buzzing was driving him crazy. He saw the thousand little barrels of cannons spitting flames in their direction. The projectiles slammed into the car, spiderwebbing the windows. Instinctively, he backpedaled to lift the kid and sling him across his shoulders. Jorgo weighed almost nothing, and the outline of his body was already fading, as if the dream were striking him from its list of characters. Nadia jerked as she opened the door. David saw her eyebrows go up in an expression of disbelief. Then the young woman leaned against the car and opened her jacket. She was bleeding. A black stain was blossoming rapidly across her belly.

"No!" David roared. "I won't have it! This is my dream! I'm in control here! I won't have it!"

He made a desperate effort to regain mastery of the oneiric machinery quickly escaping him. It was like trying to grab a bolting horse by the mane to halt its frenzied course. The animal kept hurtling along, impervious to pain, fleeing toward the cliff at a gallop that struck sparks from the stones.

"NOOOOOOO!" he screamed, and his cry was written on the night in great red letters. The nightmare retreated for a moment, like a junkyard mutt taken briefly aback by someone even louder. The stain immediately vanished from Nadia's belly. David pushed her inside the car while Zenios started the engine. The vehicle peeled away from the sidewalk, door open, Jorgo's legs still dragging on the pavement. Straining his muscles, David pulled the kid's body onto the seat. The little motorcyclist was sticky with blood. The light from a police car lit up the entire street. The cops had lowered their windows and were shooting at the fugitives. Zenios clung to the wheel; between each shot that punched through the chassis, his teeth chattered. David patted his pockets for his drugs, but came up empty. The nightmare was hot on his heels now; he couldn't let himself get scared a second time. He could hear it running right beside the car with heavy strides, slamming its head against the door to force the car off the road. *I can't control a thing anymore*, David noted with a shiver of terror. Jorgo lay heavy on his knees, dead, leaking blood on the seat, staining it red. Nadia had collapsed, her face waxen; he couldn't tell if she'd been wounded again. David checked his wrist, trying to make out the digits on the blood-smeared depth gauge. *Christ!* If he ejected at this depth, he'd be pulverized before he hit the surface. The pressure would crush him like a steam hammer. He couldn't give in to nightmare, couldn't afford to wake up before he'd brought the dream world back to a normal depth. But the gauge was still stuck at 66,000, as if the oneiric submersible lay wrecked in the silt of an ocean chasm.

As the car exited town, he felt his muscles melting away under his clothes, the lines on his face altering, the square set of his jaw fading away.

"I—I'm being torn away," he murmured, hoping Nadia would hear. He dug his nails into the backseat to try to escape the tremendous suction pulling him toward the surface.

"Nadia!" he whimpered, wriggling in his too-big clothes. "I'm ascending!"

"No!" the young woman screamed. "You can't leave us like this! Bastard! What about Jorgo? What about me? You have to fix this!"

"Fix this" was the last thing he heard. Then his body broke through the roof of the car, flying like an arrow toward the vault of the sky. Suddenly, the pain was horrendous. A crushing, dismembering sensation. For a moment he thought he'd been sheared in two by a shark lurking deep in the black waters, and only the top half of his body was still trying to reach the air. *I'll never make it*, he thought, and then a hand cleft the water overhead and grabbed him by the hair. It was Marianne.

[14]

The Raft and the Medusa

He lay wrecked amid the sheets like a castaway tossed up on a strand by the final waves of a tempest. He wasn't in pain, but his body felt broken, shattered. If he could've, he would've felt his ribs with his fingertips to make sure they hadn't been mangled by the reefs alongshore. He couldn't feel a thing anymore save for a great absence filled with vague, short-lived shooting pains. The pressure had annihilated him, crushed him. No doubt not a single bone had been left intact. No doubt his skeleton was now a mere pile of splinters nothing could ever glue back together. He lay limp, a quasi-corpse of drooping flesh in the middle of a bed devastated by dream convulsions. A great big doll, a straw-stuffed puppet; the only thing still working was his brain.

All he could remember from the ascent was a tearing sensation. The certainty of having been skinned alive, scraped to the bone. He'd made the climb toward the surface only by sloughing off his flesh, jettisoning ballast, abandoning his organs one by one to make it up there ever faster. He'd tossed it all overboard, all the viscera so terribly necessary for a normal life, emptying himself as the sparkling vault of the surface grew closer, that patch of mercury, that mirror where the sun was shining. Now he lay paralyzed, invertebrate, a minimal life form reduced to an amebic, even vegetative state.

Marianne's face entered his field of vision once more. He was having trouble focusing, and the nurse's features seemed to warp like a medusa, a jellyfish torn between tides. She was speaking, her tiny mouth with its pinched lips moving vehemently. The words took their time crawling into range of his hearing. Sometimes they got lost on the way, and all he heard were incomplete sentences.

"You acted like a fool," the young woman hissed. "If I hadn't come by, you'd be dead by now! The bottles were empty; you hadn't had any water or glucose for almost three days! You were in a coma! Your vital functions were subsiding one by one. I brought you back to life with an adrenaline injection straight to the heart."

An adrenaline injection? The little bitch! That was why the distancing powder had stopped working all of a sudden; that was why the dream had suddenly veered into nightmare. *It was her!* She was the one who'd derailed it all with her goddamned medications! He wanted to swear at her, scream insults, but his mouth remained closed. Anger crackled in his skull with no way out.

"I saved your life," she stressed. "Without me, you'd be dead.

You were sinking into a coma. Do you even understand what I'm telling you right now?"

She was shouting, she seemed about to grab him by the shoulders and shake him with all her strength. Her eyes were blazing, with anger or—? She wouldn't be crying, would she? That damned idiot! He wished he still had arms to slap her till her head came off. She kept talking, faster and faster.

"You need to be hospitalized for a scan," she said. "A blood vessel probably burst somewhere in your brain, paralyzing your motor center. I noticed you lack all tactile sensation. Or maybe it's nerve degeneration . . . I can't do anything here, and if I take you to the clinic they'll bombard me with questions. I'm your program manager, and this 'trip' wasn't on the books; you never filed a flight plan. You went under alone, illegally, without assistance, hooked up to contraband equipment that wasn't even up to safety standards! If anyone found out, you could be arrested for unlawful dreaming! We'd both be screwed! Oh, I don't know what's keeping me from just . . ."

She paced the room furiously, now and then swiping at her damp eyes with the sleeve of her lab coat.

"What were you trying to prove?" she stammered. "That you could go deeper than everyone else? That you could bring back a treasure no one had ever seen before? You're so stupid! Putting your life at risk for such trifles!"

She came to the bed, leaned over David to speak with him eye to eye. Their faces were almost touching when she murmured, "And now what am I going to do with you? You're illegally ill. If I have you hospitalized, they'll put you in a penal clinic. You've put me in an impossible situation. I should've let you drown. When I think that I saved your life, and you're probably not even grateful!"

David closed his eyes. He could at least do that much. Marianne wore him out. What did she think? That he was going to cry his eyes out to thank her for intervening? She'd ruined everything! Ten minutes from the end of the job, she'd just had to come with her adrenaline injection, switching the dream right onto the nightmare track, and everything had gone runaway from there. He'd been ejected right in the middle of the action, abandoning Nadia, Zenios, and Jorgo in a tight spot. He'd jumped ship without seeing to the passengers. He had only to shut his eyes to see Nadia's tensed faced lifted toward him. There was hatred and despair in the young thief's face, a kind of scandalized terror. What had she said? *You can't leave us like this!* Something like that. Then she'd shouted: *Bastard! Bastard!* It was the first time she'd ever insulted him. Maybe she'd thought he was fleeing in fear, ejecting himself out of cowardice, when everything he'd done could be chalked up to the adrenaline.

"You were almost dead," Marianne gasped, close to him. "Do you hear me? I brought you back, I did. I called you several times, you didn't pick up. I got a bad feeling. I wouldn't have bothered for anyone else, I'd have tipped off the home monitoring service, but it was you . . . Do you understand what I'm trying to tell you?"

He kept his eyes closed so she wouldn't see the hatred blazing deep in his pupils; he would spare her that much, at least. Finally, she got up. "I won't say anything," she murmured. "Not right away, at least. We'll see if things improve. I'll steal some medication. I'll look after you as best I can. You'll see. You'll see."

The minute she stepped out the door, he sank into unconsciousness. He slept a long time, an idiot sleep that felt like going down a long, dark, dreamless tunnel. Whenever he came to, he would find Marianne at his bedside. First she washed him like a baby, and he was happy not to feel her skinny hands on his naked body; he would've felt like a chicken was crossing his belly. Then she would make the bed, tuck him in, turning him into a respectable patient. She accompanied all these tasks with repetitive monologues that always came back to the incredible intuition that had compelled her to slip into David's house with her oneiric assistant's master key. She dwelt in detail on the sight he'd been: pale, waxen, thinned by fasting, breathing slowed to a harsh whisper, heart beating only irregularly . . . She'd thought him dead indeed and had been this close to fleeing, then she'd recovered her composure and grabbed her kit. First an injection, a shot right to the heart to kick-start the weakened muscle. The machine had slowly groaned to life, then the heartbeats had gotten faster.

"And you came back," she concluded gently. "I spoke to you, encouraged you, and you opened your eyes. I was so happy I cried."

What an idiot, David thought, whom weakness had exempted from hypocrisy. Between two monologues, Marianne would vanish into the kitchen to whip up some soup she would then try to make her patient swallow through a straw. When he drooled, she would wipe his chin and chide him gently.

This ordeal lasted almost three days, and then she had to go away to assist another dreamer on a deep dive, someone famous whose works sold well . . . and for high prices. Even then, she found a way to slip away and see David to make sure all was well. "Do you realize what you're putting me through?" she said with a sad smile. "I'm navigating in illegal waters here. If there's the slightest hitch with the guy I'm supposed to be assisting, they'll toss me in prison for the rest of my days, and then what would become of you, eh? My poor dear . . ."

She tended to elaborate on this theme with increasing frequency. She would describe the artists' hospice in the former marble depot where Soler Mahus had been transferred as soon as he'd stopped producing marketable works. She spoke of the open dormitory and the beds with their straps that David knew well, the far-from-charitable nurses who often left patients to marinate in their own urine. Wasn't he lucky, to be pampered in his own home, his pillows fluffed daily, getting shaved and powdered?

"Now, now," she said, placing a quick kiss on his brow, "you know you have nothing to worry about. Marianne's watching over you, even if it gets her in trouble."

And off she would go, leaping into a taxi to rejoin the diver she'd abandoned mid-trance. True, she had a lot to lose if her little stunt got found out, but David couldn't have cared less . . . or so he told himself.

When she was off duty, she virtually moved into the apartment, washing her underwear in the bathroom, moving from room to room in a nightgown or pink pajamas. She would hum, yawn, stretch out her skinny arms. She had taken up the detestable habit of monologuing out loud, involving David in moronic discussions wherein she'd answer for him on the pretext that she knew exactly what he was thinking. It had become one of her refrains: "Oh, I know what you're thinking, you think that—"

In the afternoon, her chores polished off, she'd sit down beside David and read to him. At first she'd sat obediently at his bedside, on a straw-bottomed chair, and then she'd planted her butt on the edge of the mattress. Now she lay completely on the bed, a foot away from him, and he foresaw with horror the day she decided to lift the covers and slide in beside him. In such moments of extreme disgust, he was grateful for the debility that deprived him of all tactile sensation. He could tell that in a week or two, she'd stop using the guest room and come sleep with him, like a mistress . . . or a wife. It was inevitable.

She would come and lie down after selecting from the library shelves a little spy novel wrapped in tissue paper. She'd start reading, puffing out her cheeks sometimes, interrupting her reading to comment on the inanity of the plot. How could anyone take pleasure in this kind of reading? Wouldn't he prefer a nice historical novel? One of those very French stories that instructed you in the ways and mores of the past and improved you even as they entertained? David wished he were deaf, so as to be spared this unbearable chatter. Besides, she couldn't read worth a damn. She rattled off her sentences like a man cutting kindling, in a sharp voice that soon turned oppressive.

Luckily, David slept a great deal, and this anesthetized awareness freed him from the torture of living with Marianne. Alas, he dreamed no more. His sleep consisted merely of a suspension of existence not far removed from nothingness. Holes he fell into, a sheer drop, like a dead body wrapped in a bag and tossed off a cliff.

This ersatz couplehood drove him crazy. He even began to suspect Marianne of prolonging his condition to keep him at her mercy, like a pet entirely submissive to its master. He ground his teeth when she called him "my illegal patient," and when she showed up triumphantly bearing the basin of warm water and pink sponge for his wash. Trapped, he was trapped. The bed had been turned into a raft; around it, an enormous venomous medusa circled ever closer. He had to settle for drifting and waiting while trying not to think too much about what would happen next: if he never got the use of his body back, if Marianne grew tired one day of playing nursemaid, if . . . he blamed himself a thousand times over, cursed himself, accused himself of not knowing what he was doing. Why, instead of insisting on bringing back objects, hadn't he ever, JUST ONCE, tried to grab Nadia bodily and bring her back with him to the other side of the mirror? Yes, if he'd held her tight against him instead of grabbing those stupid bags of gold, wouldn't he have been able to bring her back to the surface? He spent whole hours obsessing over this harebrained hypothesis. He pictured Nadia surging up from the deep, toppling into reality in the shape of an anthropomorphic ectoplasm. Yes, he would've suddenly woken up next to an extremely fragile statue. A statue of a woman with extraordinarily soft skin, a ghost so smooth, so transparent, that he wouldn't have dared lay a finger on her. He would've left her there, as if on a pedestal, white and luminous like a consecrated host shot through with light. He would've gazed upon her from morning till night without touching her, to avoid hastening her wilt. He wouldn't have sold her, just kept her for himself, selfishly, to revel in the sight of her. He would've been the first dreamer to produce a realist sculpture, a work that represented something. A body . . . Nadia's body. A body carved from a gigantic petal, housing not a single organ. Immaterial flesh that nothing weighed down. Yes, he would've preserved her here, in the dark; she would've been his sleeper, eyes forever closed. She wouldn't have withered away for a very, very long time.

But no, that was stupid! Dreams only ever produced figurative objects, abstract eclosions . . . *scrambled eggs*, as the fat museum watchman so poetically put it. Besides, why bring back Nadia? Why inflict on her the withering that reality would bring? Once withered, she'd have to be handed over to the garbagemen, he'd have to make his peace with knowing she was interred deep in a freezer. No, she was better off where she was this very moment, deep in the dream, alive . . . *lifting her head toward him and shouting: Bastard! You can't leave us like this!*

Immobility weighed on him. Suddenly, as though he'd spent his life shriveled deep into a chair, he felt like walking, running. Maybe Marianne was the one who induced in him this desire for flight? Marianne, who shared his nights now, dressed in a sober flannel shirt. She came in smiling, with an apple and a book.

"It's easier to watch over you here," she'd explain. "The guest room is too far away, something might happen. I feel better when I'm here . . . and so do you, right? No shame in admitting it, you know."

She would lift the covers and slide under the sheets, taking care that her shirt didn't ride up her thighs, so shyly there might've been something touching about it, had her presence not been so unbearable. For a few nights now, she'd undertaken to educate David and introduce him to the pleasures of "quality reading." In the voice of a schoolmistress, she'd read him pages from an enormous historical novel recounting the adventures of the Maid of Orleans. From time to time, she'd stop, lift her head, smile vapidly and say, "Good, eh?" If he could've, he would've spit in her face.

He loathed finding her there beside him on the pillow when he opened his eyes. Over the course of the night she would sprawl out, embarking on an assault of the mattress. It was not unusual for her to fling an arm and a leg across David, as if to make him hers. More and more often, he found himself succumbing to the illusion that she'd been there for years . . . and would never leave. He even began to envy the solitude of the hospice at the marble depot. At such times he would yearn for the tiny enclaves demarcated by the rough curtains, the flimsy beds with their straps, the neglected patients, Soler Mahus, who was ending, in utter public indifference, a life wholly consecrated to the art of dreams. When would David join him? Most likely the day Marianne was caught red-handed, absent without leave, for she neglected other divers ever more often to see exclusively to him, her patient.

"Phew!" she'd declare, barreling breathlessly into the apartment. "That big lummox has gone under for a good week! We'll have some time to ourselves at last." She, who once spoke so little, never stopped talking now.

But the hardest pill to swallow was still how she would ritually punctuate her soliloquies with the words: "It's nice, just us, isn't it?" To escape her diarrhea of the mouth, David tried to cut himself off, but his brain did not respond well to requests. With each new attempt, David felt like he was piloting a bomber bashed up by AA guns. A bomber losing altitude, its cockpit filling with smoke . . . Had he contracted the notorious porcelain disease Soler Mahus had spoken of? Was the world down below fossilizing inside the hemisphere of his brain? That was a diver's number one fear. Too rapid an ascent was known to provoke a kind of cerebral hernia that dream characters suddenly found themselves prisoners of; it was said that when these curious porcelain tumors were dissected, tiny, exquisitely chiseled figurines were found inside—an entire microscopic world that fit inside a matchbox. Surgeons appointed to autopsies collected these malign excrescences, which, like geodes or Kinder Surprise eggs, contained every character the dreamer had ever imagined. Quite a market had developed for such items; there were even swap meets. Was that how Nadia would wind up, on a shelf in some surgeon's library, reduced to the status of an amusing curiosity showed off to friends over for dinner?

"Look at the little woman hiding behind the car—yes, the one waving that little revolver around! Marvelous, isn't it?" The guests would pass the magnifying glass around to scrutinize the miniature. Good God, yes, it was extravagant. What detail! And the little fossilized world would be the delight of colleagues in the forensic service, eliciting sharp cries from the women and ecstatic swearing from the men.

Had his hands worked, David would have palpated his cranium at length to detect any possible porcelain hernias. He knew he'd come back up much too fast, all because Marianne had deemed it wise to bring him back from the dead. All because of that idiot . . .

It didn't do much good to get worked up now. Perhaps if he remained calm, very calm, he'd speed up the healing process? He didn't put much stock in it. True, Marianne hadn't given him much reason for hope. She'd recently gotten ahold of a portable scanner and used it to take some rough x-rays of his brain.

"It's not a pretty sight, darling," she'd concluded. "There's an ugly-looking bloody effusion."

David could not repress a shiver inside. Was she about to let him die for the simple pleasure of watching over him until his final sigh? He had no doubt she was capable of it; she was crazy. He wanted to cry out for help, but who would've heard him? Nadia, lost in the depths of dream, could do nothing for him; as for Antonine, the plump baker, Marianne had skillfully gotten rid of her a week ago by announcing stiffly that "Mr. David was in a deep trance, and disturbing him for a mere trifle was out of the question."

No, he was well and truly alone on his raft, prisoner of a medusa as vigilant as she was venomous, and he saw no way of escape.

[15]

Escape

The phenomenon occurred while Marianne was away. He was lying in bed, stiffer than ever, when he seemed to hear a knock at the door . . . Not the door to the bedroom, or even the apartment, but a door situated somewhere in the back of his skull, just about at the nape of his neck. *The back door*, he thought instinctively.

The sensation was strange, unaccountable. Three swift knocks, soft and light, followed by three more, louder and harder . . . then three quick knocks again, barely grazing the wood. The rapping traveled the bones of his cranial vault like curiously rhythmic pistol shots. Right away, he was assailed by an image: a door at the far end of a shadowy hall, behind which shone a blinding light. Someone was on the other side of that door; the twin blots of his or her feet could be seen in the sheet of light spilling across the floor. Someone was knocking mechanically, tirelessly. Three light knocks, three heavy knocks, three light ones . . . *an SOS!*

It came from a great distance, and David could tell without difficulty that behind that door lay an abyss. Someone was trying to call him, establish communication—someone from the world down below. But it was impossible! It had never happened before, in the past. Had he, in his infirmity, been compensated with new powers? He clung to this idea as sweat began to glisten on his cheeks. He should be walking toward that inner door, clutching it by the knob and trying to open it. But he was exhausted, and fell asleep before making it halfway down the corridor. The next day, he remained alert all day, but alas, no light went on in the back of his head. Blinded by the gloom, he failed to locate the door and refrained from moving, terrified at the thought of getting lost in the labyrinth of his cervical convolutions. Now he kept his eyes permanently shut to cut himself off from the outside world, scrutinizing his own private night in hopes of seeing the dot of a keyhole winking at him from the dark. He heard the SOS again, two or three times more, without being able to situate it. When Marianne came back, he refused to take the medication she persisted in putting on his tongue. She scolded him like he was a child, but he didn't give her a moment's thought. He was afraid the drug would weaken his ability to dream. Wasn't the door the sign of a trance in the offing? Not for anything in the world did he want Marianne to suspect a thing. He was going to escape! Someone was digging him a tunnel so he could flee this maimed body. The possibility set his heart racing, dragging him to the edge of exhaustion, and Marianne spent a sleepless night watching over him, certain he was going to have a heart attack.

For three days and nights he remained on the lookout, hoping insomnia and fatigue would sharpen his senses and ease the passage. He'd often noticed that states of extreme tension made the wall between dream and reality strangely permeable. If you knew how to choose your moment, you could slip between the bricks in the wall and conquer the obstacle. Sometimes he heard knocking at the door, and at other times he detected pickax noises, as if someone were digging an endless tunnel in the back of his head. He alternated between phases of excitation and despondency. He felt like a man buried alive in the coffin of his body. Reality weighed on his chest and belly like the layer of earth between an entombed man and his headstone. There was no side door; salvation could only come from below. Someone would soon reach him, pry the nails from the bottom of his coffin, and let him out. Oh, how he wished he still had enough sensation in his skin to detect the scratching of tools under his shoulder blades. He had to keep hope alive: any minute now, the trapdoor would open, and he'd vanish like a rabbit into the depths of an illusionist's hat.

Marianne circled the bed, frowning, suspecting something was up. He tried to pull the wool over her eyes by affecting a weary expression, but she didn't seem to be buying it. He kept his eyes closed all the time to get used to the inner dark and remained sitting in a corner of his skull for days at a time, waiting for the ray of golden light to spill at last from under the mysterious door. The SOS rattled the jambs with disturbing vehemence, and he wondered if Marianne might not hear it. He lived in terror of her suddenly suspecting him of trying to escape; he knew she was well capable of resorting to the most extreme means for holding on to him. Would she think twice before trepanning him with her own hand? He wasn't so sure. The night before, she'd brought over a kit of surgical instruments and lined them up carefully in a drawer. What was she getting ready for? If she found the door inside, wouldn't she be tempted to bore through his bones and stitch it shut? He could picture her quite clearly, blocking the hallway with great lengths of catgut, leaving him no chance of escape . . . He had to flee before she decided to take action.

Luckily, by groping around in the darkness, he managed to locate the door and begin making his way over. The closer he got, the more violent the SOS became. The fist behind the door was getting impatient. The blows resounded through the labyrinth of his half shut-down brain like a gong echoing in a train station. He walked with his hands outstretched and seeking, but the hallway was endless, and it took him a century to reach the porcelain knob. When his forehead hit the door with a hard smack, he froze, his breath short.

"David," whimpered a voice from the other side, "is that you? You have to come . . . everything's going wrong."

It was Nadia. He didn't know how she'd gotten all the way up here, but was that remotely important? What counted was that she'd come looking for him, that she'd shown him the way.

His hand closed over the porcelain knob. It was smooth and icy as a stone egg. He turned it. The void sucked him in right away, and he began to whirl down into the deep without holding himself back in any way, or even trying to slow his fall.

[16]

The Emigrant

David walked toward the edge of the garage to survey the landscape. He felt exhausted, and his whole body hurt. Over the last few days, he'd worked like a maniac to try to repair the worst damage, and without the sturdy body he'd gotten used to wearing in his dream world, he'd probably have died at the task.

When he'd arrived, he could tell right away Nadia hadn't been lying. Everything was going wrong indeed. The dream world was still stuck at 66,000 feet, and it was clear the pressure was beginning to close on it like a vise, crushing its edges, its borders, its very cosmos.

"When you ejected, everything got stuck," Nadia had explained. "We were still prisoners of the great deep; here and there, the walls sprang leaks. That's why I set out to find you. You're the owner; you're the only one who can fix it. People down here say you have an obligation to maintain things in good working order; it's in the lease."

All it had taken was a quick stroll for David to notice all around him the groaning of the hull's abused metal. The pressure of seawater on the vault of the sky had deformed it, denting it like an old car. The blue was flaking from the effects of damp, the clouds rusting. Everywhere, water was seeping between the reinforced plating and the bolts—salt water, which tarnished all it touched. The empty lot had become a muddy waste where starfish swarmed by the hundreds. The damned animals had mounted an assault on the city, scaling buildings, slipping through windows, exasperating the citizens.

David had made his landlord's rounds, holding Nadia by the hand. But the young woman remained distant, sulky. He could tell she still held his hasty departure against him, as well as Jorgo's death. Though he'd explained it wasn't his fault, that Marianne had triggered the nightmare with her damned injection, Nadia remained suspicious and aloof.

The sky really looked terrible. Like an aging hull letting in water. Worst of all were the rusted clouds, which only moved now with a creaking noise and a shower of red dust. To top it all off, the air reeked so thickly of silt that it made him gag. The streets were empty, everyone lying low at home in hopes that living conditions would improve. David and Nadia walked through the empty streets of a ghost town entrenched in its funk, stepping over starfish crawling over the sidewalks.

"They snuck in through cracks in the hull," Nadia murmured. "They're colonizing the bathtubs, coming up through the drains."

The most worrisome part was the damp in the bulwark. It blistered the sky's paint and was slowly dimming the sun. Already less bright, the star had taken on an ugly yellow tinge, and when it shone, it gave off smoke that smelled like a sputtering candle. He had to do something right away, plug the leaks and caulk up the heavens before a bulkhead gave way to flooding, let loose a deluge.

David called for general mobilization and put up the highest ladders he could find. For a . . . week? the populace made fire lines to pass buckets of tar and welding alloy. The vault of the sky was reinforced with stays and beams that didn't look very pretty, but relived the hull's ribs of the terrible pressure upon them.

"Why not just bring us back up to a less dangerous depth?" Nadia suggested.

"I can't anymore," David confessed. "My body's out of commission up there. I don't have the same powers as before . . . Something's broken."

"Oh," the young woman sighed impatiently. "You always did like being begged."

But that wasn't it. David really felt a stiffness taking over. Even his dream body didn't feel as supple, as strong as it used to. It was now a somewhat inconvenient outfit that rubbed him wrong at the seams. A coat too heavy to wear. Things themselves were overtaken by a certain rigidity, a sudden lack of elasticity. They no longer transformed with the same carefree joy as before. So it was with the starfish. He'd been unable to check the sudden spread, and now they were rotting, letting off a horrible odor—they seemed to exist *outside of him*, against his will. Independently of his desires. But this waning of his powers wasn't his only worry. There was also Nadia. Nadia, who was suddenly distant, as if irked to see a bothersome guest make himself at home. And everyone shared in this irritation, slowly bringing David around to feeling like a spoilsport.

"You're never going up again?" Nadia asked. "You mean you're staying here for good?"

"Of course," the young man would insist. "Why go back to an uninhabitable body? You know what they're going to do to me up there? When Marianne's had enough of playing home nurse, she'll commit me to the dreamers' hospice at the marble depot. I'll rot away on a cot next to Soler Mahus, until my brain decides to wink out completely. Don't you think I feel better here, with you?"

Nadia would smile halfheartedly and press herself against him, but her body had that rubbery texture again, the feel of a dream not fully under way.

"You won't ever have nightmares again?" she would ask, over and over.

"No, the real nightmare is up there, lying in wait. Whatever happens down here is nothing compared to what's waiting for me up there, see? Here I can walk, I can talk, I can make love."

She nodded, pensive.

"Your skin," David finally asked. "What's wrong with it? It's like rubber."

"Oh," she shrugged, dodging the question. "We're all like that now. It must be because of the moisture. A way of staying waterproof . . . but the pink is pretty, right?"

They walked through the streets. Now that he'd plugged the leaks, the starfish were dying by the thousand, blackening the sidewalks with their marine rot.

"Will we start pulling jobs again? Break-ins, and all that?" Nadia murmured. "Like before, I mean?"

David wasn't sure. Burglary seemed incompatible with his new status as landlord. Wasn't he here to restore order to a world in critical condition? Wasn't he a sort of doctor-architect? They expected efficient solutions from him, plans, responsible management. Hell, it wasn't going to be easy to ensure the safety of this microworld trapped at a depth he could do nothing about. A thief? No, rather a guardian, a sentinel.

"Don't you think we'll get bored?" Nadia would say. "It's sort of bourgeois, don't you think? A living-room life. What will we do if we don't rob people?"

She didn't seem to be swayed by this new side to things. She took no pride in David's sudden responsibilities. "Plus, my feet hurt from all that walking," she declared with a pout.

Jorgo lay in the back of the garage. He was dead, no doubt about it, but his body was otherwise unchanged. When you walked up to him, his eyes began to move, but no sound escaped his lips. He was like a big, somewhat cumbersome doll that you were afraid of leaving alone, but whose presence made you ill at ease after just a few minutes. Maybe a nuclear suppository would've improved his condition, but where would you get drugs like that down here, and without a prescription, to boot? Nadia spoke to the dead man as if to a child, and insisted on giving him sponge baths. David wished he could've said that kind of attention probably annoyed a dead body, but he was afraid the remark would put her in a bad mood again. After all, wasn't it his fault Jorgo had died?

While she lathered up the corpse with a pink sponge, he went out for a walk. Strangely enough, ever since he'd moved into the dream as a landlord returning to his property after a life of absences and voyages, he'd felt vaguely like a fraud . . . an emigrant. And yet he was at home here, wasn't he? He was the one who'd created this world, these people. In a way, he was their god. So why were they snubbing him? Because he'd come from Reality? Because they found him too different?

He walked three laps around the world, head tilted upward to keep an eye on the cracks in the sky. Passersby did not say hello. They even drew back as he went by, as if to keep from touching him.

"Is that the guy from the real world?" he heard once, behind his back. "His skin sure is a weird color."

He walked on, dragging his too-heavy, too-massive body along. Rusted old armor with insubordinate joints. What was he hoping for? Exhaustion that would thrust him into sleep and make him forget his cares? But coming all this way just to sleep was stupid.

In the papers, they accused him of defacing the environment with the hideous girders he'd put up to support the sky. They expressed astonishment that a former thief could pretend to tell respectable people how to behave. Certain scandal sheets insinuated that he'd been ousted from Reality for shady reasons. They portrayed him as a wheeler-dealer working for people on the Surface. *Are we to let ourselves be governed by an outsider?* barked the headlines.

David paced to and fro, ill at ease. Even Nadia no longer satisfied him. For some time now, he'd been wondering about her. Was she really mysterious, or just skin-deep? Didn't her opacity hide a profound, irremediable emptiness? Until now they'd only ever kept company during a heist. Her long silences, her refusal to talk about herself had seemed to him mysteries full of charm. Now that he was living right beside her, her opacity began to annoy him. The mystery became suspect. What if, in reality, Nadia was but a cardboard character from a genre series? One of those heroines drawn in broad strokes? A shadow puppet cut from paper far too flimsy . . . He was afraid of getting bored with her. Afraid of hearing her say the same words all the time, make the same gestures, the same faces. He was the one who'd created her, of course, but only in the context of a serial dream . . . Nadia could not exist outside of action. He'd thought about fleshing her out, giving her memories, a past, buried loves, but what would become of the magic of discovery if he already knew everything about her before she did? This dilemma drove him mad. Sometimes, when he embraced her, he felt like all he was holding in his arms was a drawing, a figure cut out from a magazine ad. A woman so thin she could've slipped through a mail slot. Could he really hold it against her? She was but one of his creatures, a quick sketch, a profile, a head of hair, a certain quality of silence and brusqueness. Secretly, he would make up a childhood for her, an adolescence, an early failed marriage with a lummox. A washed-up boxer, maybe . . . But what was the point of implanting these facts in the young woman's head if her attitude wouldn't change anyway?

Besides, he wasn't even sure he could still pull off a trick like that. Ever since he'd started living inside the dream, his powers had grown weaker. He was melting into the crowd. Becoming ordinary.

"How about we pull a job again?" Nadia would whine when they came together at night in the hollow of the sleeping bag. "Now that you can't have nightmares anymore, maybe we could start working for real?"

She clung to her role, vaguely guessing that outside her narrow remit, she wasn't much of anything.

[17]

Springtime in the Abyss

One fine morning, the flowers came up from the ground without warning. On the field of the empty lot, grass began to grow, stiff and close. Downtown, the smallest crack in the asphalt shot forth stalks of scrub still sticky with sap. Vegetation besieged the buildings, the statues. Vines covered the façade of the Museum of Modern Art, masking the windows with their hirsute cascades. Plants now hugged the vaults, festooning the sky and clouds with their villous sine waves.

"Did you do all that?" Nadia asked, yawning. "Redo the décor?"

David shook his head. For a while now, he'd been unable to accomplish these kinds of feats. He didn't know where these upheavals were coming from either.

They left the hangar, forgetting to get dressed, and ventured naked into the middle of the brand-new meadow. It was good grass: lush, well-nourished, almost insolently healthy.

The flowers were beautiful, enormous, dandling their corollas. They gave off thick aromas and sticky juices. The colors almost hurt his eyes.

"It's so pretty!" Nadia enthused. "Jorgo has to see this!"

She ran to fetch the corpse from the back of the garage and set it up on a chair in front of the door.

"It's from the starfish," she remarked. "When they rotted, they fertilized the soil, and—"

"No," David demurred. "The seawater left too much salt in the soil. The ground should be sterile by now. This is something else."

They walked through town without bothering to get dressed. No one was shocked by their nudity; they were all too concerned by the mystery of the garden that had sprung up from nowhere overnight. People everywhere were enraptured. These flowers, these colors . . . all this grass, so alive!

"It's spring!" someone shouted. "Springtime in the deep!"

The cry became a chorus, and soon everyone began to cheer for David, believing him responsible for this new improvement. He smiled modestly, not daring to protest his innocence. It was the first time everyone seemed happy about his presence.

"Wonderful," said the ladies.

"Invigorating!" decreed the men.

Children were running in every direction, scaling stalks, betting each other they could climb the giant ivy vines to the sky. Their parents had to grab them before they cleared the buildings.

"It smells nice," Nadia sighed, taking David by the arm. "Sharp, and fresh . . ."

Only when they reached the museum esplanade did the young man understand where the garden was coming from.

"It's my body," he murmured, seizing Nadia by the shoulders. "The body I left up there—it's *dead*."

"What?" whimpered the young woman, still wearing a smile.

"It's rotting," David sighed. "My rotting body is fertilizing the plants. We're growing from its compost. I—I'm dead."

"But what about . . . us? I mean, here?"

"We'll live on as parasites. We'll feed off my corpse like a flower off a dead animal. We'll start fading away when there's nothing left in the bottom of the coffin but a pile of dry bones. That's it—that must be it. I should've known."

"But . . ." Nadia stammered, "will it take long?"

David shrugged. He'd never really grasped the temporal exchange rate between dream and reality. How many weeks would springtime in the deep last? How long did it take a corpse to shrivel away within the walls of a box buried in the earth?

Nadia pressed herself against him. She was shivering. Fear had given her rubbery skin a certain human velvetiness. David placed his fingers on it with pleasure. All around them, springtime wrapped the city snugly in a fibrous, aromatic cocoon.

"Are you sure you're dead?" the young woman asked. "Is that the only explanation?"

David nodded. He knew he was right. Somewhere up there on the surface, a machine of muscle, bone, and guts had given out. The decomposition of organic matter had acted like fertilizer on the dream world. The world encysted in the diver's dead brain had begun sucking out the powerful juices of this disintegration just like a rose thriving on the spoiled meat of a dead mole.

"It's better this way," David murmured against Nadia's temple. "At least we'll have a beautiful summer."

"And after?" the young woman sobbed. "After that?"

David shrugged. *After?* What did that even mean? He didn't even want to think about it. Moments were better. This way, they wouldn't have time to get bored.

ABOUT THE AUTHOR
AND THE TRANSLATOR

SERGE BRUSSOLO is one of France's most singular, influential, and perennially bestselling authors. He is most acclaimed for novels that are hypbrids of science fiction and fantasy, set in a uniquely skewed reality. But he is also one of France's most prolific authors, producing seminal works in numerous other genres, including historical fiction, thrillers, horror stories, crime novels, and young adult fiction. Remarkably, though many of his works have been adapted to the screen, *The Deep Sea Diver's Syndrome* is his first book to be published in English.

EDWARD GAUVIN is a translator from the French. His work has won multiple prizes and has appeared in *The New York Times*, *Tin House*, *Subtropics*, *World Literature Today*, and *Weird Fiction Review*. The translator of more than two hundred graphic novels, Gauvin is a contributing editor for comics at Words Without Borders.